BLOOD MATTERS

A FAMILY BY CHOICE NOVEL

BY CAROLINE FRECHETTE

Renaissance

Cover art by Frank Formantin. Cover design by Caroline Frechette. Interior design by Natasha Brousseau. Edited by Marjolaine Lafreniere, L.P. Vallee and Evelyn Cimesa.

Legal deposit, Library and Archives Canada, October 2015.

Paperback 978-1-987963-07-6

Ebook ISBN 978-1-987963-06-9

Renaissance Press

http://renaissancebookpress.com

info@renaissancebookpress.com

To my sister Annie
I know kids can be cruel,
and we weren't always awesome to each other
But I hope that, as we grew,
I became the big sister you deserved.
I hope you know how I much love you

I roll over in bed to get closer to Julie, but I realize I'm alone. She must have teleported away already. I groan. I hate it when she leaves without saying goodbye; it starts my day wrong even before I get up. I pull the blanket over my head and settle back down to sleep some more. Maybe next time I wake up, she'll be back, and then I'll get a better start.

I hear a loud thump in Mister Lupino's room, and I sit up immediately. I rush out of bed, not taking the time to put on anything over my underwear, and run to his room to see if he's all right. He's on the floor, trying to get back up, using the pole of his IV stand as a cane. I rush to him and help him stand.

"Papa, are you all right?"

He grunts irritably and tries to shoo me away, but that only makes him lose his balance further, and I need to steady him.

"I am fine, Alex. Now go back to sleep. I know you did not want to get up, I have heard your alarm a few times."

I try for a smile. "I'm late as it is. Don't worry about me. Is there something I can help you do?"

He shakes his head, his mouth moving in an odd, irritable chewing motion, shooing me again with his hands, and I refrain from sighing. His whole frail body quivers as he sits back down on the edge of his bed, still holding himself up by the pole of his IV. I wish he would ask me for help more. In his condition, things can get pretty hard. But at this time, Rosanna isn't here yet, and the nurse that comes twice a day to take care of him won't be there for another three hours, so I can't just leave him. I sit on the bed next to him, careful not to throw him off balance. He looks frustrated, so I'm going to have to be careful about this.

"You were getting up to do something. Is there something you want me to bring you?"

He shakes his head more firmly, and I sigh, because I'm starting to get a little frustrated myself.

"Papa... I moved back here to help. A few years ago, you were telling me to trust you, and to lean on you. Please, let me return the favor?"

He looks at me sideways, his lips still moving nervously in that odd gesture between chewing and mumbling, and he tries to stand again. I do the same, helping him whenever he falters, and reach for his walker to give it to him, as subtly as I can. He takes it, waits for me to hitch his IV pole to it, and starts shuffling to the hall. I follow him, staying far enough to give him his space, but close enough to catch him if he falls. He gets to the bathroom, and gets in with his walker. I know it's too hard for him to turn around and close the door, so I do it for him, leaving it open just a crack so I can hear him if he falls, but otherwise giving him his privacy.

I lean on the wall, shivering because the floor is cold. I'm tempted to go to my room to put some socks on, at least, but I don't want to be too far away in case something happens. I left him alone last week, coming home an hour after the nurse left, and I found him on the floor of the bathroom by himself, unable to

2

get up. I haven't left him alone since. It was really hard seeing him like that, helpless and humiliated; I used to think he was the most powerful man in the world, and I still do, sort of, but now he also feels kind of fragile, breakable.

When he got the diagnosis, almost a year ago, he didn't look sick at all, and I didn't believe the doctor when he said that since he was over eighty years old, Mister Lupino's chances weren't all that good. He seemed to be doing well for a while, most of the time anyway, and I really thought he was going to beat this stupid disease. But when the cancer started to metastasize, which, I guess, is when it attacks the rest of your body, his health really started to plummet. He's lost so much weight that his skin looks like it's too big for him, just hanging on his bones. His hands have started to tremble, ever so slightly, all the time, and his limbs seem to curve in upon themselves, like they were trying to creep back into his body but weren't quite sure how to do it.

I hear him shuffle back toward the door, and I step away from the wall to pretend like I wasn't waiting for him there, quickly going to grab my cell phone from my dresser and standing in the doorway to my room, pretending to be checking my messages. I let him pass down the hall, and follow him to his room. He lets me help him up in bed without saying anything, and after unhooking his IV pole from the walker, I leave it where he can easily reach it if he gets out of bed again. He struggles with his blanket, and I let him do it just long enough so he doesn't protest when I pull it over him. I reach over to the book on his dresser, and hand it to him. It's something in Italian by some guy called Italo Calvino, about a winter night and a traveler, judging by the title. He has a wan smile for me, and pats my cheek awkwardly with his frail hand.

"Thank you, son. I am sorry to be a burden."

"You're not."

"I wished to be a family with you until my old age. I did not think it would come so very fast."

I smile at him, and pat the back of his hand. I wish I could be a little more demonstrative in times like this, but it's taken me a lot to be able to do the little I do now.

"You're not that old. And we're still a family."

He smiles sadly and puts his free hand on top of mine so that he's holding it between his. It takes him a long time to figure out what to say, too long, because by the time he opens his mouth, he gets distracted by something over my shoulder. I turn around, and see Rosanna leaning in the door and knocking on it softly.

"Hello! I am here!"

I smile and nod at her. "Good! Thanks, Rosanna. You have your pager?"

She shows it to me, and smiles. "I will be cleaning the kitchen. You have left quite a mess! That young lady of yours should learn to clean better!"

I laugh wholeheartedly, and she goes away. When I look at Mister Lupino, he's smiling in earnest.

"I am glad to see you happy, Alex. You have found a great woman to share your life. It is all I could hope for. Or almost. When will you marry her?"

I smile and stand, raising one of my hands and picking up my cell phone with my other one.

"And this is my cue to leave, before you start talking about babies again. I'll be back in the evening!"

4

He smiles and shakes his head, and I walk out while I still have that feeling that everything is back to the way it should be, the way it was before he got sick. I pull on a suit when I get to my room, leaving the waistcoat and tie; just some pants, a shirt and a jacket, and I skip shaving. I've been a little looser about my look since my facial hair has started to really come in, finally.

I stop by the kitchen when I get downstairs. It's really not as bad as Rosanna made it out to be, and I can smell she's baking something. She frowns at me.

"Alex! You are not leaving without breakfast, are you?"

I smile and sit down. "I suppose I can wait, since it smells this good."

She nods, satisfied, and starts some coffee. She doesn't look at me when she talks again, which is a measure of her discomfort.

"How is Domenic?"

"He's in a good mood this morning, I think. At least that's the way I left him."

She starts the machine and turns to me, with that expression that's sad and happy at the same time that women do so well. She walks around the counter to hug me. I let her, because it's Rosanna, and even though she was never with Mister Lupino that way, she was more the woman I thought of as having been a mother to me than Mister Lupino's actual girlfriend. She smells of baking bread and cinnamon and her home-made spaghetti sauce. As she releases me, she smiles.

"You are a good son, Alex. You are exactly what he deserves at this time in his life."

"Thanks, Rosanna. But it's easy to be good to him. He's been good to me."

5

She nods, watching me like she's trying to read something in my face, and then she turns around, going to the oven to retrieve the croissants she was baking. I just stay at the counter and watch her, because I know by now that I have to let her serve me my food, or else she gets mad.

I tap the power button on my phone for the eleventh time this morning. No missed calls. She does it pretty often, but it still makes me feel weird and moody every time she just disappears before I wake up and doesn't turn up until lunch. I know she does a lot of field work, but I still wish she would wake me up before she goes or call to let me know when she's coming back. I'm having a hard time concentrating on the things I have to do as it is, I don't really need that on top of everything.

The door to my office opens and in walks a young girl I've never seen before, no older than twenty or so, with long blond hair in a French braid and a skirt suit that's a good fit but has seen better days, which she probably got at a thrift shop. She seems surprised to see me, and a little uncomfortable, as if she really wasn't expecting anyone in here.

"Hey." I sit up straight. "Can I help you?"

"Mister Lupino?" She's a bit awkward in her question, but she doesn't ask in that dismissive, incredulous manner that a lot of people have when addressing me, as if someone as young as I am couldn't possibly have co-founded something as complicated as the Lupino-Dow Foundation for Extrahuman Studies.

"Yeah, that's me. Who are you?"

She steps toward me, holding out her hand, and I shake it automatically. "My name's Karen," she says. "Karen Mason. I'm your new assistant."

I frown. The name rings a bell. I try to dismiss it as having probably heard her name mentioned by Julie or Jill or something, but it feels like it's more than that. Like I should know her. Damn this work. It makes my mind so tired it makes me imagine stuff.

"Oh! Uh... welcome. Sorry, I didn't remember you started today."

"That's all right. I would have introduced myself earlier, but..." She trails off, and I nod.

"I get it. This place is just nuts with the amount of work. You holding up OK?"

"So far. I'm actually here about something. There's a man here who says he needs to see you."

I frown and get my phone to check my appointments. "Really? I don't remember – "

"Oh, he doesn't have an appointment. He just says he has to see you right now." She looks over her shoulder, then leans forward and whispers. "He's a bit weird, and really angry."

I sigh. She's probably afraid of sending him away. "Do you need me to go out there and turn him away?"

"Oh! No! I mean... I can do that if that's what you want. He's not that angry. He... just said you'd want to see him."

8

I raise an eyebrow. If this is someone I know, like Jimmy, or Luke, they'd have called ahead. And they've never just showed up here uninvited, so I'm pretty sure it isn't either of them.

"Did he say why?"

"No. He said it was private. He said to tell you his name is Randall Colson."

A really weird feeling comes over me, like the information goes straight from my ear to the rest of my body, starting with my feet and my hands, numbing it to the point of feeling tingly and being unable to move, until it finally makes it up to my brain. Colson. Randall Colson. Randall and Margaret Colson. Those are names I'm never going to forget for the rest of my life.

I try to talk, but the words haven't really formed in my mind yet so my mouth just works soundlessly for ten good seconds. She frowns, obviously taken aback by my reaction, which is fair. "Uh. Let him in," I finally manage to say

She nods cautiously, like she's not sure she should really listen to me. "All right. Would you like me to bring you some coffee?"

"Sure."

She leaves. I look around at the mess on my desk, and start putting things in piles. I'll have to look really hard to find the stuff I was working on again, but I don't care. For some reason, it feels kind of important to impress the man who's been the father I haven't been able to be to my son.

I'm not quite done by the time he gets there, so he sees me scrambling, and worse, he sees me stop self-consciously which signals for sure that I was doing it just for him. He doesn't seem to notice or care, just walks in, carrying a cardboard box, which he sets on the floor next to my desk, before extending a hand. I shake it, helplessly realizing that my hands are moist, before motioning to the chair in front of my desk. He sits down.

"Mister Lupino," he says. "I don't know if you remember me. We met when – "

"When I was still called Winters," I finish for him. "You and your wife adopted my son."

He nods, seeming a little bit relieved. "Actually, this is precisely what I'm here about. It's fortunate that you work at this institute... it makes you the perfect person to handle my problem."

We sit on either side of the desk, though it takes all my willpower; I'd rather be pacing back and forth. "Your problem?"

He clears his throat. "I'll get to the point. Something happened with Nicolas."

I knew it. I try not to show how nervous I am. I gave him up specifically to avoid problems, so that he could have a normal life, so that nothing bad would happen to him.

"What happened?"

"He... he put my daughter in the hospital. It's..." His voice cracks a bit on that, and I can see the distress in his eyes before he takes a deep breath, and glares at the floor, like he's trying to find the determination he needs. "He's one of... your kind."

He makes a vague hand gesture towards me, still glaring at the desk but not meeting my eyes. I clench my fists again. I know I should probably know better, and have gotten used to it by now, but it still stings when people find it acceptable, or even normal, to refer to us like we're some kind of other species, or sub-human, or something like that. And he's not just talking about me, now; he's talking about my son.

"My kind?"

He shifts, and frowns more deeply at the desk, like it's going to help him stay mad. I recognize the expression; it's one I've worn pretty often myself. "You know… all you people with… these abilities. Isn't that what you do here?"

I take a deep breath. I want to let this go, because I need to get to the bottom of what's happening here, instead of getting into an argument about semantics.

"Sort of. What happened to your daughter, and what does it have to do with my son?"

"He electrocuted her." He finally looks up at me then, and I can see the frown is still there, forced over wide, haunted eyes. "With his hands!"

I prop my elbow on the desk, and cover my mouth with my hand, leaning my head against it. He's not even six yet. I was twice that age when I first used my power, and before I seriously hurt someone with it. And even then, I had good cause. Did Nicolas have good cause? What have they been doing to my son?

"What happened?"

He looks at me, his eyes even wider. His breath is short when he speaks, and a bit shriller; I think I can feel a sort of panic mixing with whatever it is he's feeling. "What do you mean, what happened? I just told you! He electrocuted her! He's dangerous!"

I grit my teeth. I'm not liking this guy's attitude. They seemed so normal when I met them. Stable. Happy. Comfortable. I guess extrahumans really are that scary to normals.

"And you want me to help him control his power?"

"No. Yes. In a way. I want you to..." he hesitate, his eyes dropping to the desk again. "I want you to take him back."

My heart does that funny thing when it stops and starts up again, like a jackhammer. How could he just want to give him up like that, like he's not good enough anymore, like he's some kind of garbage? He's not even thinking of Nicolas; he's only thinking of himself.

At the same time... could I really get him back? And what would that mean? I've dreamed about it for a long time... Can I handle it? What if he doesn't want me? What if he's traumatized? He doesn't even know who I am.

"I... I have to think about it."

His fists clench on his knees. "No. I'm sorry, but my decision is final. I can't handle him. We can't handle him. What if it happens again? He could kill my little girl!" He looks up at me again. This time, the fear is naked in his eyes, all traces of grief and anger gone. "You have to take him back."

I lean my forehead in my hand. I feel dizzy. I want to punch this asshole, but I want my son back. How can I just decide this right now? Without telling Julie? I rub my mouth again, and feel the stubble of my beard like sandpaper on my palm. It's distracting, but not enough.

"You can't just do that to him. How can you abandon your child?"

"You did it. If you don't want him..."

"No! That's not the question! I loved him, and I wanted to give him a better life than I had to offer. That's all. You... you just want to get rid of him!"

"He's dangerous!" His voice is so shrill, he's almost screaming. "My little girl..." He shakes his head. "You take him. He's your son, and you run this institution. What other place could be better than this? Social services?"

I grit my teeth again. Social services? I've seen kids in social services. Luke takes in plenty of kids who have found themselves become homeless drug addicts and prostitutes, who have had to escape the hellholes social services put them into.

"Fine. I'll take him. When do you want to bring him by?"

"He gets off of school at 3:00 PM. I can give you the address. You can go get him. I've put his things in that box."

I frown at this, trying to remain calm. "You told him someone else was getting him, and he went to school anyway?"

"Are you crazy? There's no way I'm going to upset him! He might kill me!"

He points to the box he brought in, and I take a deep breath, flexing my fingers. It's a miracle I haven't grabbed this guy by the collar and shaken his brain out of his skull by now, but I suppose controlling anger is something I'm going to be teaching my son, if he's anything like me. Fortunately, I have Julie.

"You can't just leave him like that, without telling him why. This boy thinks you're his father. He doesn't deserve to be abandoned without even so much as an explanation."

"No way. You explain it to him. I'm through. My little girl... after what she's been through, you can't ask me to risk my life. She needs me."

I can hardly contain myself anymore. I spring out of my chair, and start hammering my finger at him, almost yelling.

13

"You listen to me, asshole. You are a role model to this kid. It's bad enough you're kicking him to the curb like he's trash, but after what you tell me happened, you and your wife are his only anchor, you're his whole world, and he's probably scared shitless right now. You explain to him, you tell him that it's not his fault, that you love him, or it's me you'll have to deal with. And you should know I'm a hell of a lot more dangerous than a scared little boy who doesn't control what he can do."

He's actually paling, and shrinking in his chair; I haven't gotten used to that yet. It doesn't happen that much anymore that I lose my temper or try to scare someone, and it would appear that I'm much more impressive as a full grown adult than I was as a teenager, superpowers or not.

He licks his lips. "You don't know what you're asking."

I breathe through my nose. "I have an... agent. She can neutralize powers with a touch of her hand. You'll be perfectly safe."

"I suppose that could work." He's sighing as much as talking right now. "His school is Tesla Elementary. I will be there by 2:00 PM."

"I'll meet you. Get the hell out of my sight."

He stands up straight, adjusting his jacket like it can give him back some dignity, and struts out of here. I sink in my chair, putting my hands on my desk; they're actually shaking, and so are my arms, and shoulders. I'm weak, and drained; anger has always given me strength in the past; it's never felt that way. Is it because I'm getting old, or because it has to do with my son?

There's a feeble knock at my door, and I look up sharply, thinking it's him, but it's only the girl, Karen, with a cup of coffee in her hand. I lean my head in my hand.

14

"Come in."

She walks to my desk awkwardly. "Sorry. I didn't want to interrupt your... meeting, so I waited."

She sets the coffee down in front of me. It's black. I pick it up, and drain half the cup. It's piping hot, but that's never bothered me. "Thanks."

"Is there anything you need?"

I nod, and pick up my phone. "Yeah. But I got it. You can go."

She seems relieved as she walks away, and I can't blame her. I bring up Julie's contact, and hit the call button. At least now I have a legitimate reason to call her.

I'm leaning on the hood of my car, staring at the school, and I haven't craved a cigarette this bad in at least two or three years. Julie rubs my upper arm, trying to comfort me, but she doesn't say anything.

The school is a big brown cement block, just like the one I attended when I was a child. I have mixed memories of school; I never made it past grade 6, so it was about 12 years ago, for me, and it all seems very distant, but the memories I do have are pretty good. I mean, I was never a popular kid; I had a temper and I was prone to fights, but I wasn't ostracized, and there was no one there I was afraid would break my bones at the slightest provocation. But I don't know what I'm gonna find here. I mean, I'm not bad when it comes to dealing with kids in pain, but I've never had to deal with one that young.

I check my phone again. He's late. What if he's not coming at all? What if he just decided to abandon him, and let us deal with the fallout? I take deep breaths, and Julie squeezes my arm. In twenty minutes, school will be over, and someone will have to step up. A woman comes up to me, wearing a skirt suit, her hair up in a bun. She's gained some weight, and there's a little gray in her hair now, but I recognize the woman who swore she'd care for my baby like he was her own. She extends a hand; I guess she recognizes me too.

"Mister... Lupino?"

I nod, shaking her hand. "Yeah. I changed my name."

She has a small, unconvincing smile. Her eyes are red, not the slightly red and puffy of having just cried a little, but the kind of blood-shot, bleary look that comes from having spent a long time crying not too long ago. "I'm..."

"Mrs. Colson. I remember you. Margaret, right?"

She nods, glancing at the school. Her eyes are filling with tears. "I... I'm so sorry about all this. It's just..."

She looks so genuinely distressed that I feel my anger ebb, and I wrap my arms around myself. This is going to be tough for Nicolas, but maybe it isn't entirely a bad thing. If these people are willing to be done with him, and if he's going to be stuck with someone that gave him up, maybe he should be with the person who did it because he was thinking of his welfare.

"I get it," I say. "You've got your own kid now, and you're looking out for her."

She has a relieved little smile even as she wipes the tears from the corner of her eye, carefully, trying not to disturb her makeup, and failing. "I just want to protect my little girl. It doesn't mean that he isn't a good boy, or that I don't love him, it's just..." Her voice falters, and she turns away from me. I see her shoulders shake a bit, and hear her breathing deeply.

When she's finished wiping her eyes and has calmed down a bit, she turns back to me. "How..." Her voice shakes, and she clears her throat. "How is this going to work?"

18

I look down. As excited as I am to see my boy again, what is he going to think of all this? Am I going to be the person he blames for his parents leaving him behind? What kind of damage am I going to have to deal with?

Julie looks at me, and decides to take over. "All I need is to touch him, and I can take away his ability for an hour or two. It should give you ample time to have a conversation with him."

She nods a bit, and walks toward the school. She heads straight for the principal's office, and we wait outside as she goes in to have Nicolas called. There's a small wooden bench there, in the hall. The walls are full of posters announcing the school end of year show, soccer tournaments, and large murals depicting the bottom of the ocean.

I jiggle my leg as I wait, no matter how many times Julie puts her hand on my knee to make me stop, and I bite my cuticles to the point of making my fingers bleed. I have no idea how much time I actually wait, but it feels like an eternity. Finally, I hear light steps echoing down the hall to my right, and I look up.

The resemblance to Lori is so striking that I find myself standing slowly, like I'm in a trance, even though I'm not consciously thinking of doing it. There's a lot of her in that face, mostly the eyes, and the mouth, but I can also see myself as I was long ago. It's the hair, exactly the straw color that mine has, and the shape of the face, but also the expression: he's frowning seriously up at me with a mixture of defiance, anger, and fear. He's taller than I expected.

He gives us a suspicious glance, and walks in the office. I follow him in, Julie on my tail. His mother, or, Mrs. Colson, is greeting him, looking at us nervously. The secretary shows her through another door, and she motions for us to follow.

19

We're shown to a small infirmary, with one cot in a corner and a small desk. The secretary leaves us, closing the door behind her, and Nicolas frowns up at Mrs. Colson.

"What's wrong, mommy?"

She tries to smile, but he isn't fooled. She clears her throat, and motions toward Julie and I. "Sweetie, I want you to meet these nice people." Julie walks toward him, big smile, hand extended. He shakes it cautiously, and I make myself do the same, though I can't seem to manage the smile. Mrs. Colson continues. "They're here about what happened with Anna."

"Oh." His eyes widen, and he takes a step back, looking at the woman he thinks of as his mother. "Are they here to punish me? Are they going to take me away?"

She pets his head, her eyes glistening with tears again. "They're not going to punish you. But they are going to take you for some time."

Nicolas's eyes widen, and he takes another step away from us. "Where?"

"They're going to take you to a place where they can help you manage what you can do. They're here to help you."

"How long will I have to stay?"

"I don't know." She forces a smile again, but even I can tell that she's trying not to cry.

Nicolas throws his arms around her, holding her tight, his voice rising, tears forming in his eyes. "I'm sorry! I didn't mean to hurt her, please don't make me go! I won't do it again I promise!"

She tenses when he touches, her, and I have to look away. I'm not someone that likes to touch, and I understand how dangerous he can be, but right now, I want nothing more than to hug him and tell him that it'll be all right, and it makes me nauseous to be watching her refusing to give him that. His crying is growing into great sobs and wails, which cut off his breathing.

"It's not about that, sweetie... we know you're a good boy. They're just going to help you get it under control."

"Don't make me go with them! I wanna go home with you and daddy!"

"I'm sorry, sweetie." Her voice cracks a bit, and she swallows. "But look. See that man there?" Nicolas looks toward me, his whole body shuddering with each hiccupping sob, wiping at his eyes. Mrs. Colson continues. "He's also your daddy."

Nicolas frowns at her, confused. "Wh-what?"

"You have another daddy, and it's this man. He loves you very much."

"No! I only have one daddy and it's my daddy!"

I step forward, trying to look reassuring. "Hey, buddy..."

He recoils from me, the sobbing starting up again, even worse than before. "No! Mommy, make him go away!"

She stands, taking a deep breath. "I have to go, Nicolas."

"No! You can't go! Mommy please, I'm sorry! I'll be good! I won't hurt Anna again, I promise!"

"I know you didn't mean to. It's going to be all right. Just listen to Mister Alex, won't you?"

She starts to walk away. Nicolas throws himself at her, gripping her skirt, still crying and shouting, but the words are so deformed I can't make out what he's saying anymore. Mrs. Colson just stares at him, not moving, tears running down her cheeks, and Nicolas just keeps getting more and more hysterical. Julie eventually has to go help, gently prying him off of his mother, because I'm just standing there like, frozen, incapable of doing anything. I watch Mrs. Colson leave, and that little stranger who is my son screaming in pain, and it looks like it's all happening in slow motion, like a movie.

Once the door is closed, I see Julie looking my way, her eyes pleading, but not without a trace of anger in them, and she's right. It's not her responsibility.

I come toward him, bending down to touch his arm. "Listen, buddy..."

He screams and gets even more agitated, trying to kick me. "Don't touch me! You're not my daddy! I hate you! This is all your fault!"

I take a couple of steps backwards, and the back of my thighs hit the desk. I lean on it gratefully. He's right, of course. This is my fault. He's my son. I made the mistake to turn him over to these people, and now I have to deal with the damage.

I hear Julie making soothing sounds, and Nicolas's screams subside into a kind of crying that at least sounds normal. I see him sort of melt against her, sobbing into her shoulder, but I don't move. I think that if I touch him again, he'll start screaming at me. I can't help but wish it was me that was able to calm him down, but it's not. I guess all I can do right now is bear the brunt of his anger, and his resentment. It's not like I don't deserve it, anyway.

APRIL 25TH, 3:45 PM

All our sundaes have melted so much they look like bowls of milk. It was Julie's idea, and I thought it was a good one, but he doesn't seem to want to eat it. I poke his melted ice cream cup and its contents spill over the side a bit.

"Not that hungry?"

He shrugs, not looking up at me. He's sitting across from me at the metal picnic table in the parking lot of the Dairy Queen. His legs are just not long enough to touch the ground, and he's been swinging them back and forth under his seat. I wait to see if he's gonna say something, but he doesn't, so I fill the silence.

"The ice cream here's not that great. I couldn't finish mine, either."

He rubs his upper arm nervously, shrugging again. His eyes are puffy and red, but he hasn't cried in at least forty-five minutes.

He looks up at me hesitantly. "When do I get to go home?"

I glance at Julie, and she shrugs. I guess she doesn't know how to handle this any more than I do.

"Uh..." I shift in my seat. "Well, not now."

"Are they mad?"

"What? Who?"

"My parents. Are they mad? Is that why they won't let me come home?"

"No. They're not... they're not mad." That is the truth, basically, but I'm not sure what I can follow that with. Saying they're afraid of him isn't better at all.

"You're not a good liar," he says without looking at me.

"I'm not lying. They're not mad. When you're a grown-up, your emotions get real complicated. I think they just don't know what to do."

He sighs and looks down at the table. "Where will I go?"

"We'll take you to my house."

He swings his legs faster, angrily. "I don't want to go to your house. I don't know you."

"Well, you need a place to stay, at least for now, right? I have room in my house. Plus your grandfather lives there, and he's..."

"He's not my grandpa! And you're not my dad!"

I raise my hands. "Ok! Fine. No problem. But we do need to help you with what you can do, and you'll need a safe place to stay for the meantime."

He doesn't answer, staring sulkily at his melted ice cream. For a while, I think he's not gonna answer, and I grab the empty cups to go throw them out. When I get back, he looks up at me with a mix of suspicion and hope.

"So... you're really gonna help me?"

I sit back down, smiling. "Yeah! That's right."

"Can you... can you make it go away?"

I want him to believe everything will be ok so bad that it's hard to tell the truth - but I'm not going to lie to him. "I don't know. I don't think so - not for good, anyway. But I have some friends who can make it go away for certain amounts of time, and with time, you'll be able to manage it so that accidents don't happen."

He nods. He doesn't look particularly happy about all this, but he doesn't look devastated, either, which I suppose is a step forward.

"When I'm better, can I go home?"

I glance at Julie, and she just gives me a sad little look. I take a deep breath, reminding myself how I'm not going to lie.

"I don't know."

He hugs himself, and he looks so tiny at that moment, it's hard to not lean down and hug him. He doesn't look up. "...they hate me now, don't they? Because of what I did to Anna? Even if I didn't mean to?"

I sigh. "They don't hate you. It's just... You know, ordinary people... people who can't do the things we can do, I mean. They get scared easy. They don't know what to do with people like us."

He frowns up at me, suddenly less shy. "Do you mean... you're like me?"

"More or less. I don't know much about electricity. Fire's more my thing."

"Fire?"

I smile. At least we're back into territory I know very well. I look around to make sure not too many people are looking, and I hold out my hand, producing a flame. His eyes go wide, and he finally looks like a normal kid at that moment.

"Wow."

I put out the flame so that we don't get seen, and wink at him. "Yeah."

He tilts his head on one side, his face screwed up in concentration. I let him think. Eventually he looks up at me gravely. "Did you ever hurt someone?"

This is something I've never been, and never will be comfortable discussing with anyone, but I can see how much he needs to hear the truth right now.

"Yeah. I did, a few times." Some of those were intentional, of course, but I've had a few accidents, and that's what he wants to hear about.

"But not anymore?"

"No, not anymore." I smile. "I learned to control it. But when I was younger, things would often start to burn when I got mad. And sometimes I hurt people, too."

"So, if I learn to control it..."

"There's a really good chance you'll never accidentally hurt anyone anymore."

He looks cautiously hopeful, chewing his lower lip. "And then... will my mom and dad love me again?"

I look down at the table so he doesn't see the pity in my eyes. I can't remember being this young, but I can't remember a time when people pitying me didn't piss me off, either.

"I don't know. I don't think that it has anything to do with how much they love you. I think it's a bit more complicated than that."

He nods, hugging himself. He's starting to look defeated again. I try to smile as cheerfully as I can.

"It's no use worrying about that right now, though. Come on. Wanna go see my house?"

APRIL 25TH, 4:27 PM

I park the car in the driveway and glance at Nicolas. He's still hugging his backpack, looking at the floor, silent. He hasn't spoken a single word since I dropped off Julie at the office. I know from experience that time does a lot to heal a person's pain, but I also know some things can leave you scarred forever. I just hope he's going to be ok.

I step out of the car, and walk over to the back door to the passenger's side. I open the door, crouch to put myself at his level, and try to be reassuring.

"Come on, buddy. I know this is hard, and the situation really sucks, but it'll get better. Won't you come in with me? You can't just stay in the car. Besides, there's someone inside who's dying to meet you. You'll love her, I'm sure."

He has a careful little look toward me, and shrugs hesitantly. I step away, waiting for him, giving him his space, leaving the door open, and after a little while, he slinks out of the car, still hugging his backpack. It's the only thing that he has left that's his, and I get how important it feels right now, even though it's probably full of homework he won't ever have to look at from a school he might never go back to. I close the door when he's clear of it, and smile, walking at his slow pace toward the house.

"So, is there anything you'd like for dinner? We can give ice cream another try if you want, but maybe we can make it more of a dessert this time, what do you think?"

He has a tiny, despondent, one-shoulder shrug, but he glances at me sideways. "...I like pizza."

That makes me grin. Maybe he will be OK, if he's worked up an appetite. "So do I. Let's go in and order some."

We walk in, and the smell of something baking hits my nostrils; Rosanna's been busy, even if I told her not to plan anything for dinner. It's hard to convince her not to do exactly as she wants where food is concerned. But what matters most to me right now is that she respect the other request I put to her: to not tell Nicolas that I'm his real dad until I say so. I know it'll be hard for her because she's been so excited and she's missed him so much, but I think I can trust her.

We haven't even taken off our shoes yet that I'm already hearing her running toward the entrance, and when she appears, she's still wiping her hands on a dish towel. She grins at us, throws the towel over her shoulder, and bends down to wrap Nicolas in a tight hug almost before she's stopped walking. I'm about to tell her to let him go, but when I see his face, I decide against it: he looks surprised, but he doesn't look scared. In fact, I think I see the hint of a smile on his lips.

"Hello, little one!" Her accent is even more musical than usual. She releases him to be able to look at his face when she's speaking. "Young Alex did not want me to cook you dinner, but I have made some cookies. I hope you like chocolate chips?"

Nicolas nods, smiling the first real smile I've seen on his face since he was a baby. Rosanna grins.

"Good! I will go and take them out of the oven. Come to the kitchen!"

She walks back inside the house, and Nicolas turns to me. "She's nice. Is she your wife?"

I laugh. I know that some people don't mind age differences, for example, Dow's wife is some ten years younger than him, but Rosanna's nearly sixty, and I'm twenty-three.

"No, she's not my wife. She's... a friend."

We get to the kitchen as Rosanna is taking cookies from the baking sheet and putting them on a plate. She smiles at Nicolas, and then speaks to me in Italian.

"He is beautiful, Alex. He looks just like you."

"Thanks." I reply in the same language; I have a feeling she's about to say something she doesn't want Nicolas to understand. I fold my arms and lean in the doorway, watching Nicolas sit at the lunch counter.

She grins at him and continues speaking in Italian. "How is he handling the news about the adoption?"

I shrug, because I don't really know how to answer. It was such a heavy moment for him, I have no idea how much of it he registered, so I haven't brought up the fact that I'm his real dad, and I have no idea how I would. She's pretending not to care if I answer, though, just serving Nicolas his cookies without looking at me. Nicolas isn't reacting, either, like he knows that this is supposed to go over his head, or he's too shy to ask what we're talking about. I decide to take advantage of the moment.

"I'm going to see Mister Lupino upstairs," I say in English, so that Nicolas understands where I'm going, and then I walk out.

I'm not worried that Rosanna will tell him anything she's not supposed to; I know I can trust her not to pressure him into thinking about things he's not ready for.

He's in bed, his back to the door, and for a moment, I think he's sleeping, but then I hear a page turn, so I walk in, knocking lightly on the open door.

"Papa?"

He turns, and has a thin smile. "Alex."

I bring the chair closer to the bed so I can sit, and he puts away his book, awkwardly, like his limbs are too stiff to move properly. I don't offer to help him, even if I want to. I don't know what to say, either, so I just wait for him to speak.

"Rosanna has told me about your son."

"I thought she might have." I don't look at him, because as much as I really need his advice, I'm afraid of what he'll say.

"She was very excited to see him return. As I was." He presses the button on the bed controls, raising the head of the bed so that he's sitting, facing me. "He knows you are his father?"

I shrug. "His adoptive mom told him. He didn't believe her, and he doesn't really understand how he could have two fathers."

"You have not explained about the adoption?"

I scratch the back of my neck, and look up at him. He doesn't seem angry, or judgmental; all I can see in his eyes is concern, though I'm not sure I like that any better.

"He's six. He's not ready to deal with that."

He clears his throat and makes that odd chewing motion with his mouth. His voice is dull, and quieter than it should be. He always sounds kind of breathless when he speaks, now. "I know you better than to think you would underestimate a child's capacity to understand."

"He's dealing with a lot of stuff right now. His adoptive parents... they just dumped him. The last thing he needs to know is that this isn't the only time that someone who was supposed to love him just gave him up to someone else."

Mister Lupino shakes his head. "It is true that he may perceive it this way. But he may also need to know that the person who did give him up as a baby has come to regret this decision, and now wishes only to have him stay. That is the case, is it not?"

I sigh. It's the truth, but it's still hard to admit. What if I get my hopes up, and then I don't get to keep him? "Yeah, of course it is."

"Then, he may need to know that there is someone in this world who wants him more than anything."

I run my hand over my ponytail. As nervous as I am, I can't help but smile. There's a reason I always go to Mister Lupino for advice; he always knows how to put everything in a positive light. I still don't know if I'm ready to tell Nicolas yet, but at least now I know how to say it in a way that might mitigate some of the additional damage I could do.

"Thanks, papa."

He waves a hand dismissively, and I manage to ignore the uneasy shakiness of his gesture.

"You do not need to thank me. Just let me meet this boy so I can see if he has remained as handsome as he was when he was an infant."

"I don't like it."

I take a deep breath and run my hand over my hair. He's just a kid, and he's going through some heavy stuff right now, so I can give him a break, even though I've just spent the last two hours fixing up the room for him while he was getting acquainted with Mister Lupino and Rosanna.

"What's wrong with it?"

He shrugs. "It looks like a grandpa room."

I look around. It's true that the antique wallpaper, with the oak bedroom set and the brown comforter kinda make it look like an old man's room, but that's mainly because it's Mister Lupino's furniture.

"Yeah... it kinda does. But it only has to be for tonight. Tomorrow, I can go buy you new stuff."

He frowns at the ground. "So... am I gonna stay here for long?"

I rub my hands together, as if the gesture can give me some courage. Maybe the time has come to make things clear. I sit on the bed so I don't have to be looking down at him.

"Nicolas..."

I hear the faint, almost inaudible pop which signals Julie's arrival in the hallway, and I'm flooded with relief at the realization that I get to put off having this conversation. I stand and poke my head out in the hallway, and she notices me before getting in the bedroom we share. She changes course, and comes to hug me.

"Hey, handsome."

I close my eyes and breathe in her scent, and for just a second, everything feels normal again. "Hey."

"You OK?"

I shrug, and look over my shoulder. Nicolas is standing a bit further back in the room, in his room, and he's looking at us curiously. Julie follows my gaze and smiles at him, walking in.

"Well hello there, cutie!"

He frowns at her. "Hi."

She keeps smiling, in that awkward fashion that I've seen people do when they have no idea what to say; I just never thought I'd see that expression on her face. I'm simultaneously relieved that I'm not the only one that feels this way, and anxious that she's not going to be able to help me much in that department.

"So!" She says after a minute of awkward silence. "You're all ready for bed?"

He shrugs. "I didn't brush my teeth."

"Don't worry about it," I say. "We can skip today. I skipped doing it for like, five years, and I was fine."

He frowns, and looks down with a tiny nod. "OK." He turns to the bed apprehensively.

"Everything OK, buddy?" I ask. He mumbles something in response that I don't understand. "What?"

He glances at me sideways. "I don't have Mr. Gordo. I never sleep without Mr. Gordo."

"Who's Mr. Gordo?"

"He's my piggy."

I look at Julie, realizing I completely forgot to ask her. "Did you bring the box? From my office?"

She bites her lip, making a face. "Sorry. I didn't think about it. But!" She smiles at Nicolas. "I might have something for you."

She disappears, and comes back about a minute later holding the stuffed bunny that used to belong to Nicolas, the one I salvaged when my condo exploded and kept with me all this time. I look at him to see if he'll recognize it, but he seems to have forgotten it just as surely as he forgot me. He was too young.

"What's that?"

"It's a bunny." She smiles proudly. "It used to be very important to –"

"To me," I interrupt her. I know she hates it, but it's late, and I've already made up my mind that I wasn't having this conversation tonight. "It helped me get through a lot of bad dreams."

Nicolas frowns. "But if you give him to me, won't you have bad dreams?"

I shake my head. "I don't need him anymore. But I think you might. I want you to have him."

He takes the bunny, hesitantly, staring at it for a long time before he answers. "What's his name?"

"He doesn't have one, actually. Why don't you name him?"

"I can't do that. He's not mine."

"He is now."

"OK." He nods gravely, like I just told him he was the only one who could save the world. "Thanks."

APRIL 25TH, 9:24 PM

Julie and I both breathe a sigh of relief when I close the door to Nicolas's room after putting him to bed. I turn to her and she puts her hand on my cheek.

"How are you feeling?"

I shrug, and start heading for our bedroom so that Nicolas doesn't hear us talking right on the other side of his door.

"I don't know. I haven't really had a moment to myself today." I sit on the bed to take off my socks.

"Hmm." She sits down next to me on the bed, leaning back. "Does he still thinks he's going home?"

"No."

"Have you told him about the adoption thing? That you're his real dad, and the other people aren't really his parents?"

"No."

"Hmm."

I hear disapproval in that little noise, and before I know what I'm doing, I'm making excuses. "There wasn't time. And he wasn't ready."

"He wasn't, or you weren't?"

I feel like glaring at her, but I don't have the energy, and I don't really want to argue. She's right, anyway. "I guess I wasn't."

"Why not?"

I shrug, but she doesn't say anything, so after a while, it becomes obvious I have to answer her question. "What if he freaks out? What if he hates me for abandoning him as a baby? What if it hurts him more?"

She still doesn't say anything, only purses her lips and waits for me to go on. She knows me well enough to know it's not the whole story, and in all the years she's shared my home and my bed, she's gotten almost as good as Mister Lupino at dragging it out of me.

"What if he doesn't want me?" I say, after a long silence. "Or what if I tell him, and he's happy, and then I have to give him up again?"

I sneak a glance at her. I know it's not like her, but I still dread seeing pity in anyone's eyes, especially hers; but she's only smiling when I look up, like she's happy about what I said.

"What?"

She shrugs. "You don't have to worry about any of that stuff." She reads my answer on my face, because she replies before I have time to formulate it. "What I mean is, sure, maybe he might react badly at first. You can do your best, but that sometimes can't be

40

helped. But he'll come around. And why would you have to give him up?"

"I don't know. What if his parents take him back? I mean, there were contracts, and everything, and the lawyers were pretty clear that I was giving up my rights forever."

"Don't worry about that. They're the ones who dumped him, I think they lost their rights. And if it does come down to a legal battle, we've got Dow on our side. He might be absentminded these days, but he's still really good."

"Yeah." I sigh. "And... what about you?"

"What about me?"

"You're OK with all this?"

"Of course I am." She smiles. "Why wouldn't I be?"

"I dunno... it kinda means you're a mom, now. Well, sort of."

She blinks, and laughs. "I hadn't thought of that! I guess it's OK."

"You sure?"

"Yeah. Why? Did you think I would freak out?"

"Well... you said you didn't want kids."

She waves a hand dismissively, a bit like Rosanna does, and I find myself wondering if you can pick up someone's gestures by living with them. It makes me hope I'm picking up something of Mister Lupino's, something that'll stay behind when he goes.

"That was five years ago," she says. "I'm almost thirty now, things are different. Plus, he's already grown past the staying up all night crying and diapers full of poop stage, so that makes it even better."

I smile. This feels like the first thing that's gone well since the beginning of the day. "Thank you."

"Hey, don't worry about it. I love you, or I wouldn't still be with you after all this time. Can you imagine how bored I would be? I'm never bored with you."

I grin, and kiss her. She starts unbuttoning my shirt, slowly, and deliberately. When she releases my mouth to kiss my neck, my fingers curl around the cloth of her shirt to lift it up, almost automatically. It's been a long time since we've done this; she used to want to all the time, and, honestly, so did I, but since we moved back in here a couple of months back, we haven't had a lot of chances.

"Hmm... what are you doing?"

I can hear her grin; there's a slight sound, like a very mild rustling, the sound of her skin folding. "I'm undressing you. What's it look like?"

"I thought you didn't want to be heard..."

"We can be quiet... Didn't you want me to be a mom?"

I smile, until it dawns on me what she's saying, and I push her away to look at her. "Wait... what?"

"I was only kidding." She smiles again, and then pouts when she sees I'm not amused. "What is it?"

"Well, don't you think we should talk about this?"

She pulls away from me. There's a tiny part of me that's disappointed, but most of me really wants to know what she's talking about.

She sighs audibly. "Way to kill the mood again. Sheesh. Sometimes I wonder what the hell I'm doing with you."

"Don't do that, Julie. What do you mean? Do you... do you want to have a baby?"

She shrugs, not looking at me, and I start to sweat and feel cold all at the same time. She purses her lips, and thinks for a while, before turning a challenging face on me.

"So what if I did? What would you do?"

I blink, and stare at her, dumbfounded. What would I do? I have no idea. "Uh... I dunno. I mean... we already have Nicolas, and..."

She snorts, and shakes her head. "So, what, you expect me to raise somebody else's kid, and be a mother to him, but never want any of my own?"

"That's not what I said. And that's unfair. Give me at least five minutes to think about it, can't you?"

She shakes her head and sighs, leaning her face in her hands. "Never mind. I don't know what I was thinking. It's probably nothing. Just PMSing, that's all."

"Julie... I'd be glad to have a baby with you, just... well, now might not be the right time, you know? We have a lot on our plate."

Now, maybe it's me not being fair to her. I'm the one that has a lot on his plate, not her. I guess she doesn't have to deal with all that, but at the same time, what the hell prompted this?

43

"You know I don't expect you to do anything about Nicolas, and if you're uncomfortable..."

"I'm not uncomfortable." She shakes her head. "That's not what this is about. I just... well, I never really had a family before."

"Neither have I."

"Then, you understand, don't you? Doesn't it give you ideas? I mean... A kid. You and me."

I take her hand, and squeeze it in mine. I have a thought for Lori, and Nicolas, when he was a baby. I thought I had a family then, but with hindsight, I'm not sure how far we would have gotten, Lori and me. I'm glad it's Julie; I'm glad I met her, and I'm glad she's in my life now. I just don't really know how to say that. Fortunately, she appears to share the sentiment, and she leans in to just snuggle with me, resting her head on my shoulder.

"Don't worry," she says. "I really was kidding. For now, at least. How about we start with a dog?"

APRIL 26TH, 1:26 AM

At first, I'm not sure what I hear. Then, as I wake up more and more, the sound becomes clearer, if not exactly louder: it's definitely a kid, crying. For a few seconds, I have no idea where it could be coming from, and then it hits me, all at once, like a flood, everything that happened today. Nicolas.

I rush out of bed, and half-run to his bedroom. I open the door so fast I feel a rush of wind around me, and Nicolas hears me, grabbing his blankets and letting out a strangled little shout. I stare at him, but he doesn't seem upset, just scared at my sudden appearance.

"M-Mister Alex? What's wrong?"

I watch him. He's not crying, his cheeks are dry, and apart from the fright, he looks sleepy. "Nothing. Are you all right?"

"Um... yes. Why?"

I can still hear the sound, but he's still not crying. It's not physically possible for him to be making this noise, not with me standing this close and looking right at him: he just looks calm, though slightly worried, and his mouth closed. His shoulders should be jumping up and down with the great big sobs I'm hearing.

45

"Nothing. I thought I heard... something."

He lies back down, still tense, as I exit the room. No one else could be making this sound, no one else has that light a voice in this house. So if he's not crying, what am I hearing?

I had a big day. I'm probably just tired, and it's playing with my mind. I try to sleep and ignore the sound, and the fact that it only seems to keep getting louder.

It feels good to be getting to the office. Not that there is anything going on there, but it's a relief to get away from home, so I don't have to think about the state Mister Lupino's in, and Nicolas... He's my son, and he's at home, and I should be wanting to spend time with him, but I can hardly stand myself when I'm with him. It's like it drains me completely, of everything. Besides, he likes to be around Julie better, so I'm doing him a favor, in a way.

When I get to my office, there's someone in it that I don't know, and for a moment, I just stand there, wondering if I got lost. The first week we had this new building, I kept getting turned around, because there are too many offices, and most of them are not used yet. She blinks up at me, looking nervous, and I remember where I saw her.

"Hi. Um…" I wave my hand in front of me, like that's going to help me remember her name.

"Karen," she supplies quickly, catching the cue. She seems slightly annoyed, but she's faking a smile through it. I guess maybe she can work for me, if she's able to stop her annoyance from showing that well. "My name is Karen."

"Right. Sorry. I've had kind of a weird night."

"I heard." She has the decency to look troubled. "I was just doing some tidying up. I hope it's all right."

I take a look at what she's doing. She's been picking up the papers that fell all over the floor yesterday, and I can see she's making little piles, sorting them in some sort of fashion. Looks like my work will be a lot easier.

"No, it's fine. Thanks."

I sit on the guest side of the desk, and I watch her go at it. She's pretty efficient, and concentrated. I had a few misgivings about her at first. I mean, she's a bit weird. She's wearing make-up, and high heels, and it's been a really long time since I've seen anyone dressed that way: she's wearing a pink skirt suit that looks like a hand-me-down, not fitting her so well. It's like she's trying so hard, though all the girls I work with dress more casually, or even sloppy, like Julie. Her hair is pulled into a ponytail, but it's not even, there are bumps and bits of hair sticking out, like she doesn't know to use a brush. It's weird that she's a girl and I can make a better ponytail than her.

I'm starting to get that same weird familiar feeling I got when I first met her. She feels my eyes on her and lifts her head, frowning at me.

"Is something the matter, Mister Lupino?"

"Please, call me Alex. And... I don't know. Do I know you from anywhere?"

She frowns, and flushes, like I've said something troubling, or embarrassing. "Oh, I don't think so!"

I watch her for a little while longer, but it only seems to make her uncomfortable. Besides, I'm not placing her from anywhere else, and it might just be the Nicolas thing throwing me, like when I was hearing voices last night.

"Sorry. Probably imagining stuff. I haven't had my coffee yet. I'll go and remedy that."

She puts down the papers she has in her hands, and she hurries to beat me out the door. "Oh, no, please, allow me! It's part of my job!"

I blink at her, and give her a small nod to say that it's OK. I've never had an assistant before; I had no idea they fetched you coffee. Turning around to look at the mess, I can sort of see why she'd be so enthusiastic, though. It has got to be easier than trying to sort out all this junk. At least, it's better than it was before.

I walk to sit behind the desk, just staring at the papers, which she distributed in neat piles in an order that I don't understand. What if I can't find anything anymore after she's done ordering it? I'm already overloaded with work, can I afford to lose time finding my stuff? I'm suddenly reconsidering the wisdom of my idea to come in and work. Is this really more comfortable than being at home?

There is a slight knock at my open door, and I look up, expecting to see Karen, but it's Dow standing there, looking concerned. "Hey, Alex. You all right?"

I nod, and he walks in to sit across the desk from me.

"I just ran into your new assistant in the break room. She looked a bit frazzled, and she told me you were here, so I thought I'd check it out. I really didn't expect to see you here today."

"I'm fine. What do you need?"

49

"I don't need anything. How is your son?"

I shrug. "Fine, I guess. I left him with Julie. She's helping him get settled. She gets along with him better than I do."

He nods. "I see. And you didn't want to stay and... spend time with him?"

I shake my head. "It's no use. I mean, he's getting used to me, but... well, he's sad."

"Ah. Yes. It can get hard. I know that when my own daughter is sad, there is not much I'm good at. My wife handles all of that."

I don't know Dow's wife very well, though I do see her every once in a while, but I know she's good with kids. The main reason I don't see her often is because whenever we have a party, or function, she's always looking after Dow's four-year-old daughter. Is this what my life is going to be, now? Or Julie's life? Spending all our time looking after kids?

Karen walks back in holding a cup of coffee carefully, staring at it, taking slow steps, obviously careful not to spill it. She lowers it to me, never taking her eyes away from it, and seems intensely relieved when I pick it up.

"Can I... get you anything else?"

I frown, drinking my coffee. I might be the co-administrator of the center, but it doesn't mean I'm used to bossing people around. She just stands there, waiting for me to say something.

"Uh... that's all. Thanks."

She nods, and turns around. "I'll be in my office. Page me if you need me!"

I watch her walk away, taking a sip of my coffee. She put cream and sugar in it, so it's vile, but I need the coffee right now, so I drink it anyway, and turn my attention to Dow.

"Where did you find that girl?"

Dow watches her disappear down the hall, and shrugs. "I dunno. Jill takes care of HR. Ask her."

"Is she one of us?"

He raises an eyebrow at me. "You're starting to sound like them."

"Like who?"

"The normals. You know, us against them... we have to try and break down that mentality."

I roll my eyes. "Doesn't just calling them normals make you sound the same?"

He heaves a long, heavy sigh. "I guess. To answer your question, yeah, I think she is. She does something with water, I think."

I keep sipping my coffee, thinking. Water with fire. I wonder if Jill did it on purpose? We stay silent for a while, and Dow's voice is a little quieter when he speaks again.

"How's your father?"

"Same, I guess."

"I heard he was getting worse."

I frown, downing the rest of my coffee and putting the cup down on the floor for lack of space on the desk. I suppose it makes sense he would have heard, after all, his mother is dating

Mister Lupino, but it doesn't mean I want to discuss it. Dow should understand. He's old, like, forty-five, and his own father died some fifteen years ago; he should know it's not a comfortable topic for discussion.

"Yeah."

"If there's anything I can do..."

I start picking up the papers left on the floor. "Nope. Not a thing. It's all good. I got work to do."

He sighs, but stands. "Of course, you do. Call me if you need me. Don't work too hard."

APRIL 26ᵀᴴ, 5:47 PM

When I get in, I see that the glass doors leading to the salon are open, so I walk to go close them. I feel oddly protective about this room: it's where I had all of the most meaningful conversations I had with Mister Lupino, all except for the very first one. Even when he's gone, I don't want anyone in there, anyone changing anything about it.

When I'm close enough to the door, I hear voices inside, and I peer in. Nicolas is sitting on my chair, leaning his head in his hands, frowning down at the marble chess board. Mister Lupino is sitting across from him, his walker, IV and oxygen tank pushed as far as they'll go behind his chair, as though if he doesn't have to look at them, they're not really there.

"Take your time," Mister Lupino is telling him. "Each piece you move changes the board, and gives or takes away opportunities for your other men."

I stand there, frozen, watching them. I was older than Nicolas is, a teenager, and Mister Lupino wasn't sick, but other than that, this is like watching a memory of the first game we ever played. I take really shallow breaths, afraid to make the slightest sound and disturb them, shatter this image. Nicolas picks up a pawn between his thumb and forefinger, and pushes it one space forward, frowning in concentration, like it's the most important move he'll ever make, and I know it feels that way. Every move does, when you're playing against Lupino.

I feel a hand rub up against my upper arm and come to rest on my shoulder, and I start. I'd been so absorbed I never even noticed Julie come up to me. I glance back at them, hoping I didn't make too much noise, that they didn't notice, that the moment isn't broken, but they're both looking at me. Mister Lupino is smiling warmly, and if it weren't for the bathrobe and the tubing escaping from his nose and arm, I'd think there was nothing wrong with him; he looks so happy. Nicolas looks reserved and wary, and definitely not happy to see me.

"Alex, my boy! You are home."

I reach out to give Julie's hand a light squeeze before walking in the salon. "And you're out of your room. I have to say, I could get used to that."

I touch his shoulder, lightly, because he gets hurt easily, and he smiles and pats my hand. "I have been playing with young Nicolas here," he says. "He has your talent for chess."

I laugh. "Come on. He can't be that bad."

Lupino smiles. "Do not underestimate yourself."

I turn to Nicolas. He seems a bit happier too, more relaxed, watching us interact. He sees me look at him, and he turns to point to one of the pictures above the mantelpiece, the one that shows a younger Lupino, with his dead son and wife, from long ago. "Mister Lupino says he has a son that was called Nicolas, like me," he says.

"Nicola," I correct instinctively. "It's true."

"So was he your brother?"

I open my mouth and close it, unsure how to answer. The right answer is yes and no, Nicola was Mister Lupino's actual son, who died before I was born, and I can only wish I was related by blood to this amazing man who decided to make me part of his family just a few years ago.

Julie sees me hesitate, and steps forward with a smile. "Dinner's ready. How about we go and eat? We can talk about all this complicated family stuff later."

Nicolas frowns, and looks at me. I don't answer, so he just follows her out of the salon. Mister Lupino doesn't watch them go; instead, his eyes are on me, frowning slightly, in that air of deep thought he sometimes has when he's deciding something. I let him think it through, because if I speak first I'm going to say something stupid and antagonize him, and I don't want this moment, one of the first good ones we've had in a long time, to be ruined any more than it has to.

"What is it that you are waiting for?" he says.

"What do you mean?"

"You know what I mean."

I sigh, and sit down in the chair Nicolas had just been occupying. "Just... give me some time. I don't want to add to everything he's going through. You know that."

"You will add to it. If you wait too long, you will just prolong it."

I sigh and hang my head. I suppose he has a point, but I don't want to talk about it. Fortunately, he's always been really good at reading my signals, and he doesn't press the issue.

"Let us go see what Rosanna has left us to eat. I have had a good day today, and it has left me with quite an appetite."

I stand while he very slowly and carefully gets up to his feet. Something bright and pink catches my eye right outside the doors, and I take a look. There is a child there, standing with her back to us, her shoulder-length blond hair tangled and dirty. She's barefoot, and wearing nothing but a faded pink cotton nightgown. I take a step toward her, frowning.

"Hello?"

Mister Lupino bumps me accidentally while grasping his walker, and I see him frowning in the direction of the girl, then at me. "Who are you talking to?"

I turn back to point out the girl to him, but when I look again, she's not there anymore. I frown. "Did Nicolas have a friend over?"

"No. Why?"

I shake my head. All the stress must be really getting to me. Maybe this is just a part of getting old that nobody talks about.

"It's nothing. Let's go eat."

I sit up straight in bed when I hear it, my heart pumping. I've never heard a higher-pitched scream; it's coming from outside the room, and it is definitely a child's voice. I run out of bed, throwing the blankets off of me, not caring about Julie's startled gasp. I make it to the door to Nicolas's room before the scream stops. I'm sure it was coming from there, it had to be, but as I put my hand on the knob, I hesitate. What if it's the same as last night, and it wasn't him screaming?

Still, I have to make sure, so I turn the knob carefully, and push the door open as slowly and quietly as I can manage. It's dark and silent inside, and, just as I thought, Nicolas is lying in bed, sound asleep, his breathing even and slow. I stare at him for at least half a minute. Could it be he had a nightmare and screamed, and fell back asleep?

"Alex? What's wrong?"

I start, and turn to see Julie, walking toward me, holding a bathrobe around herself, her hair messy and her eyes puffy.

"Did you hear that?"

She frowns. "Hear what?"

I stare at her. She seems utterly confused; maybe she didn't hear the scream. Maybe there wasn't anything to hear. I shake my head.

"Nothing. It's nothing."

"Nothing? You ran out of bed like GenEx was at the door. What's going on?"

"I think I had a nightmare. It was..." I think back how that scream made my ears hurt, and I was awake. "It was real vivid. Anyway, it's over now."

She purses her lips, and I can tell she doesn't quite believe me. I can't blame her; I don't believe me either.

"OK," she says, but I know she's just humoring me. "Let's go back to bed then."

I nod, and follow her quietly. She takes off her robe and snuggles next to me, but all I want to do is just hold her, and even that I do half-heartedly. She eventually falls asleep curled up against me, but I don't close my eyes again that night. I'm starting to wonder if it isn't more than just being tired.

APRIL 27TH 7:36 AM

Julie stirs in the bed as I'm finishing to button up my shirt. She crawls up to me, and runs her hands up my back, resting them on my shoulders.

"Where are you going?"

I turn to give her a smile that I hope is convincing. "Work." She snorts and moves away from me, aggressively. She doesn't say anything but she's clearly sulking. I sigh. "What is it, Julie?"

"What's so important about work that you have to go in again today? Why don't you take a few days off to deal with all this?"

I frown at her. "Our work is important. You know that."

"Yeah, I know that. I also know that there's nothing going on right now that'll really suffer from you taking a few days off."

"You don't know that. There might be something urgent going on that we don't know about."

She rolls her eyes. "There are these inventions, I know they're fairly new, but they're called phones. You can let someone know

59

about something over a distance, by text or voice, instantly! I'm actually pretty sure Dow knows how to use them."

I glare at her. "What's the matter with you? What does it change in your life if I go in to work or not?"

"Because you seem to think you're more important than me. You go off to work, and I can't, because I'm stuck here. I can't just leave the kid because he'll kill your dad if anything happens, and I can't take him with me if I go to work."

"I'm not more important than you. Just... well I'd stay if I could make sure he doesn't hurt anyone, but that's your ability, not mine."

She throws her hand up in annoyance. "So what? Because I'm a null, I'm going to be stuck being his babysitter for the rest of my life?"

"Oh, so it's that bad taking care of my kid? Weren't you the one who was all like, 'we should have more kids' just the other day?"

"It's not about him. You have to see that this is just not gonna work long term."

I take a deep breath and let it out slowly. "Yeah. I know. I'll figure something out, OK? Just give me some time."

She snorts. "Yeah. Right."

"For fuck's sake, Julie, what is it now?"

"Do you think I'm naïve or something? Do you think I'm the only one that hasn't figured out you run away to work just so you don't have to deal with all this? 'Some time' my ass. You're just going to do the same as you're doing with the fact that you have to actually have a conversation with him, and you're gonna ignore

60

it until it goes away or blows up in your face, and guess what's gonna happen first."

I stand up. "What the fuck do you want me to do, huh? Whip out a solution from my ass? I don't have one. You can either let me figure one out or you can bitch about it all day. What's it gonna be?"

"Fine. Whatever. Figure something out. But when you come home tonight, I want you to have done at least something. Or I'm not staying around tomorrow."

"Fine!"

I grab my jacket, and walk out of the room without giving her a chance to say anything more. When I walk out into the hall, I see Nicolas peering out of his room, wide-eyed and nervous. I take a step toward him, but he runs back in, closing the door. It takes all my willpower not to kick something, and even then I know that it's only because I realize how much worse it would make everything. I can't believe how shitty a parent I am, after just two days of having him here. Even when I avoid him as much as I can, I seem to fuck up.

APRIL 27ᵀᴴ, 8:24 AM

I'm surprised to see Karen is already here when I get to the employee room. She's made coffee, too, which manages to impress me despite the frumpy, ill-fitting pants suit she's wearing.

"Good morning, Mister Lupino!"

"Hi, Karen."

She has two cups ready. She picks up the milk, and I take a step forward. "Is that for me?"

"Yes! You seem tired. I thought you could use it."

"I take my coffee black. Thanks, though."

"Oh! Of course. Here you go."

She picks up a cup and hands it to me. I drain half of it right there. When I'm done, I see she's watching me curiously, and I remember that most people aren't as immune to heat as I am.

"Uh, I really needed it."

She nods, and picks up the pot to refill my cup.

"Mister Dow was looking for you. He asked me to let you know as soon as you came in."

"Thanks."

I find Dow in his office, frowning over a stack of papers, holding one up and looking over his glasses, then through them.

"You need a new prescription."

He blinks, and puts the paper down. "Alex! Yes, you're probably right."

I sit down on the other side of his desk. "You wanted to see me?"

"Yes. There are a few things we need to discuss."

"That's good." I sit down. "There are a couple of things I want to ask you too."

"What is it?"

"Well... it's about Nicolas. Right now, Julie's stuck at home taking care of him, and, well... she's going nuts. I think we need a more permanent solution."

"Oh. Yes. Yes, that would make sense."

"I thought about sending him to school, but..."

He nods, understanding without me needing to say it, in a rare moment of perceptiveness. "That wouldn't do. If his powers are as out of control as his adoptive family described, an accident could happen."

"Yeah."

"But he needs an education, and Julie needs her freedom back."

"Exactly."

"Hmm." He opens his day planner, and makes a few notes in the already-full "to do" list at the bottom of today's date. "I have some ideas. I'll investigate them and get back to you."

"OK. Thanks. So... what did you want to see me about?"

"This." He pulls a stack of papers out of a pile, and pushes it over to me. "I need you to sign these."

I pick up a pen automatically. As co-administrator of the center, and Dow being a lawyer, I'm used to signing the stuff he hands me without reading it. This one catches my attention, however, with having the word 'adoption' at the top. "What's this?"

"A petition for adoption. For you to adopt Nicolas." He frowns, suddenly concerned. "You do want to... keep him, don't you? I assumed... if I'm wrong – "

"No! No, you're not wrong." I take a deep breath, looking over the papers, though I'm so nervous my brain can't process what I see. "Just... why do I need this? He's my son."

"Well, yes and no. Technically, when you gave him up, you gave up your rights forever. So... you have to sort of... adopt him back, if that makes sense."

"But I still have his birth certificate."

He sighs. "It's just a formality, Alex. It doesn't involve that much trouble, and I'm taking care of everything. I've already gathered all the paperwork, and filled all the forms. All you have to do is sign it, and then there might be a home study."

"What? What's that?"

"It's a social services thing."

I put down the pen, my mouth going dry. The fear of social services has been ingrained in me so long that it's hard to disregard it right now. "OK. I don't want to be involved with that."

"Alex..." He picks up the pen, handing it to me again. "There's nothing to worry about. I've got this. I'm there for you. I'm your lawyer in this, and it'll be fine."

I yank the pen out of his hand, clicking my tongue. "Don't patronize me."

I try to read over the document, but the legal language, and how many thoughts are floating around in my mind make the letters swim around, and the words lose all meaning, so I just sign, and push the papers back to him. He nods and picks them up. "Great! Now that you... where are you going?"

I stop before I'm out the door. "Back to my office. We're done, right?"

"Well..." He picks up another sheet of paper, and I groan. He frowns at me and puts the paper down. "You know what? Yeah, we're done. I'll deal with this."

I purse my lips, and consider staying and hearing him out, just for a moment, but then decide I've got enough shit to deal with right now. If this was an emergency, I know he'd tell me.

"Fine. Talk to you later."

APRIL 27TH, 2:39 PM

The house is very quiet when I get in. I call out for Julie, but she doesn't answer, so I guess she's gone. I take off my jacket and hang it, before heading toward the kitchen to get a snack.

I hear a light thumping, like someone's running, right ahead of me. I frown, undoing the first buttons of my shirt. "Julie? Are you there?"

There's no answer again, so I look around when I walk into the kitchen. The sound suddenly comes from right to my left; I whip my head around to catch it, and see some movement from the corner of my eye, as if someone just ran out of the dining room. I walk in there, not hurrying; I have this weird feeling of dread, like I'm not going to like what I see when I find it.

When I reach the dining room, there is someone standing in the doorway leading to the den. It's that same little girl I saw yesterday, still wearing that faded pink nightgown, her back toward me. I walk to her.

"Hello? Who are you? What are you doing here?"

She turns her head slightly, as if she's almost, but not quite, looking at me over her shoulder. Her messy hair is hiding her face.

I frown and take another step forward, but suddenly, she disappears into a ball of fire so strong it knocks me back, and I fall on my ass, my arms held up in front of me. I know the fire won't harm me, but it's still startling. When I open my eyes again, the walls and ceiling are burning, and I instinctively lift my hands to absorb the fire, put it out. I'm so surprised when it doesn't work that I just sit there, dumbfounded. This has never failed me before. What's going on?

"Alex? Are you all right? I heard shouting."

I look sharply to the side, toward the kitchen. Jeanine is standing there, her white hair in a bun, and her hands held nervously together in front of her. She's got this worried look on her face. I look back at the dining room, and the fire is gone, like it was never there. There is no trace of the girl, either. Jeanine is standing next to me by the time I've made it to my feet. She frowns up at me, touching my chin lightly with the tip of her fingers like she's examining me. She's acted like she's my mom, ever since she started dating Mister Lupino, and honestly, I've never had a problem with it. Besides, I have it on good authority that she's a pretty good mom.

"I'm fine, Mrs. Dow. I just... I'm just tired."

"You're so pale! You look like you've seen a ghost."

I stare at her, trying not to gape. She put her finger right on it. I hadn't even considered it, which is really weird, since I have superpowers and I know for a fact that vampires exist. It's a ghost. Of course, it's a ghost. I never had the impression that this place was haunted, but then again I've never lived here until now.

I smile at Jeanine, which is suddenly a lot easier to do. "I'll be fine, Mrs. Dow. Really. Thank you."

APRIL 27TH, 8:47 PM

Julie plops down on the couch next to me, sighing. She glances at the TV; I know it bugs her when I watch it on mute, so I turn it off.

"He's asleep?"

She gives me a sidelong glance, and she doesn't say anything. She hasn't said anything all evening, just entertaining Nicolas when I wasn't able to really talk to him, and definitely giving me the cold shoulder. Fortunately, I know what this is about, and I have the solution.

"I talked to Dow today." She raises her eyebrows at me, but remains silent, so I go on. "I told him about the problem of you being stuck taking care of Nicolas all the time. He said he had ideas, and he's looking into some kind of... school replacement, I guess?"

She visibly relaxes, almost like I can see the anger leaving her body. "Oh. That's good."

"Yeah."

She leans her head on my shoulder, just like that, like nothing was ever wrong, and it makes me smile. She grabs the remote from my hand, and turns on the TV, raising the volume, and zapping away from the infomercial I'd been watching to some sci-fi show apparently about two brothers fighting some kind of mystical monster. I watch in silence for a few minutes, and decide to seize the occasion.

"So, do you think ghosts are real?"

She snorts, at first, but then seems to think about it. "I dunno. I guess it makes sense. There's a lot of weird stuff in the world. Why?"

"I was just wondering." She keeps watching me instead of the TV, so I know she's not done. "I... I've been seeing and hearing things that don't make a lot of sense."

"Like what?"

I let out a deep breath. "Like... sounds. Movement. That sort of stuff." I consider saying more, but when I catch sight of the worry in her eyes, I'm glad I didn't. "It could just be that I'm tired."

She holds my gaze, but after a while, she just shrugs, as if she's dismissing her concerns. We go back to watching TV like nothing's wrong, but I can't concentrate on what's going on.

APRIL 28TH, 3:47 PM

The coffee's growing cold in my mug, but that's OK; it's the third one I've had today. I check my phone again, and frown when I see the time. I thought for sure Dow would have been in by now, but I haven't even been able to find him. Karen was no help either, but I can't blame her. She's only been here a few days; it's normal that she doesn't know much beyond making coffee and filing stuff yet.

Julie wasn't too bad this morning, but I'm still dreading coming back to her with nothing tonight, so I've called Dow a few times already, hoping he's found a solution. I'm coming home late tonight and it would sit much better if I had good news for her.

I see him passing through the hall in front of my door, and I call out to him, getting up. Fortunately, this is one of the eighteen minutes per day where he isn't too absorbed in his thoughts or whatever it is he's doing to notice the outside world, and he stops, looking in my direction.

"Oh! Alex. Can I do something for you?"

"Yeah. Didn't you get my messages?"

He digs his phone out of his pocket, and powers it on. "Sorry, I forgot to turn on my phone. I was in court."

I frown. I don't remember there being anything he was working on that would have taken him to court, and I know we have a few of his lawyer friends on hand for our extrahuman legal defense and support league.

"In court? What for?"

"A complicated case."

"That doesn't sound too good." I motion for him to step into my office, and he does, looking around as he unbuttons his jacket to sit.

"It's not too good. Wow, that girl of yours really did a great job in here. You can see the desk and the floors and everything."

I sit across from him. He's wearing one of his nicest suits, which also can't be good. Usually he can barely be bothered to shave, but today even his hair is impeccable.

"Yeah, she's pretty good. So, what was the case about?"

Dow sighs, running a hand through his hair, mussing it a bit. "It starts with an incident involving a minor. She made a lot of people very uncomfortable."

"Uncomfortable how?"

"She gave them nightmares. A sort of collective nightmare where all her friends were trapped. It's kind of a complicated story."

I frown. "That really doesn't seem that complicated a case, though."

"It's not. The complicated part is what happened after. The school got pressure from the other parents, and passed that pressure on the school board, and..." He takes a look at my face, and I guess how irritated I am with everything right now must be painted all over it, because he clears his throat and decides to cut to the chase. "Well, they're demanding that extrahumans not be allowed to register in public school. The government is looking into a way of making this happen. They're talking about a registry."

I frown. "What, like a list of what people can do? Don't they already have that? I know they already have that."

"Evidently. But this is different. It would be accessible to the public. A bit like... the sex offender registry."

I give him a level look. "You have got to be kidding."

"They're not comparing us to sex offenders. It's not that. It's... well, all right, I agree that it's bad," he says, sagging in his chair. "The problem is..."

"Yeah, I know what the problem is. I can see the worms in that can." I sigh, leaning my head in my hands. If this goes forward, it opens the door to a whole world of discrimination and persecution, and it might lead exactly down the road of the disaster we thought we avoided five years ago.

Dow raises his hands in front of him. "It's all right. I got an injunction preventing the registry from getting formed. Now all we have to do is be as proactive as we can, and really keep a lid on all the extrahuman activity before anyone else gets hurt." He stands. "I know you've got a lot on your plate right now, so don't worry, I'm not going to ask you to contribute unless it's absolutely necessary. But I might be hiring more people."

"It's OK. You can count on me. Just let me know what you need."

73

He nods as he walks out. "I'll let you know."

I watch him leave, and he's already gone for a few moments by the time I remember what I wanted to ask him. It's too late now, though. He's got more important stuff to deal with than my family's personal problems.

APRIL 28TH, 8:17 PM

The bar is a dive, as they always are. The floor is sticky, and looks like it's never been washed; I can't even be sure of what it's made of. There's a faint smell of beer mixed with vomit and urine, and even if it were still light outside, the windows are dirty enough that wouldn't let much light through.

There aren't a lot of people, mostly a bunch of middle-aged guys drinking by themselves, so I spot Jimmy right away. He's in a booth in the corner, and he nods at me when I meet his eye. I make my way toward the booth, glancing around to make sure everyone is really as uninterested in us as they seem.

Jimmy and I started meeting in places like these when I left Lupino's organization and he picked up where I left off. I used to go to his place, until Dow pointed out that keeping up a friendship with someone who was involved with a criminal organization might not be the best idea ever, that it could be used against me. He even suggested that maybe I shouldn't see him at all. But Jimmy's been my best friend since I was a teen, which feels like pretty much my whole life, and he's always had my back. There isn't much in the world that would make me drop him entirely. So we started meeting in random dives and strip clubs, always a different one, so we wouldn't be noticed.

I sit at the booth across from him, and he motions the bartender for something. I let him; I always have a drink or two when hanging with him, but never more than that. It makes him happy to see me unwind a bit, but I'm still wary of getting drunk.

"Hey, Alex."

"Jimmy. What's up?"

"Meh, same old, same old. How's the old man? Still kicking?"

I look down. It's never been a secret that Jimmy and Mister Lupino didn't get along well, but they always had some sort of respect for each other, and Jimmy started asking about Mister Lupino's health when Lupino retired.

"Yeah, he's still around. He's pretty tough."

"You still with that girl?"

"Yeah. You?"

"Well, I ain't with your girl, obviously." He grins.

"Real funny. What else is new?"

He shrugs, and doesn't answer. We've fallen in the habit of mostly talking about my business, because his is secret, and mine usually involves a few really interesting stories. This time, though, I can't think of anything entertaining or interesting, because Mister Lupino's condition and Nicolas coming back are pushing everything else out of my mind. Well, everything except for one thing, and I guess that's kind of interesting.

"You believe in ghosts?"

He raises an eyebrow but doesn't answer right away; the bartender shows up at that moment, putting down a beer in front of me, and Jimmy waits until he's out of earshot to talk again.

"Ghosts? I dunno. Probably. Why?"

"I think Mister Lupino's house is haunted."

He chuckles, shaking his head. "Seriously?"

"Yeah. I been seeing some pretty messed-up stuff."

He raises his eyebrows. "What kind of stuff?"

"You know, creepy, horror-movie kind of stuff." He smirks at me, and I roll my eyes. "OK, maybe not your kind of horror movie. But you know, a haunted house kind of horror movie."

"You're serious, aren't you?"

I feel my smile waver, and shrug, looking away. "Yeah, I am."

"Fuck. You're actually scared."

I glare at him. He's always known which buttons to push, but at least I'm not thinking about my bigger problems anymore. "Shut up. I am not. I'm…. spooked. That's all."

He kicks my shin under the table, grinning like a fool. I can see he's missing one more tooth than he was last time I saw him. I frown at him. "What?"

"I'm totally enjoying this," he says, his grin broadening. "It's been a long time since it's happened."

"Since what happened?"

"Since you'd needed my help with something."

I raise an eyebrow, as he downs a shot of whiskey. "You can help with this? How?"

"Well, I can ask Erik. I'm sure he'll know what to do. He's dead, after all. That would make anyone an expert about that stuff, wouldn't it?"

I take a sip of my beer, feeling myself relax. "I hadn't really thought about it that way, but I guess you have a point. Thanks, man."

He nods, still grinning. "Sure. I'll have him give you a call."

APRIL 29TH, 1:35 AM

Julie's lying next to me, snoring softly and mumbling about ordering Chinese food in her sleep. I haven't managed to get to sleep. It's not the fight that I had with Julie, and it's not even the fact that I noticed Mister Lupino zoning out a lot more than usual this evening. I think it's Nicolas. He wasn't as stressed, or nervous as he had been before. He laughed today. At something Julie said.

It should make me happy that he's feeling better, that he's gaining confidence and trust. But it doesn't. What if he gets attached, and something goes wrong, and he's taken away from me? What if I can't handle being a parent? What if he only gets attached to Julie, because I don't know how to be around him?

I sit up in bed, sighing. There's no point. I just keep thinking about it. Might as well get up. I pull on some sweatpants, and walk toward the door.

There's an odd flickering light coming through the half-closed door, and I push it open all the way, stepping into the hall. There is fire everywhere, in small but resilient flames, and everything that isn't currently burning is blackened like charcoal, like the fire's been going for hours. I stare at it, blinking, but I don't even attempt to put it out. I know that it's the ghost, or whatever it is, doing this: I can't even feel heat, and it's not because I'm immune to it. Even if it doesn't affect me, I can usually sense heat, sort of like an echo of what I can do, something that's an extension of me. But there's nothing there, no real fire. I suppose it makes it a lot less frightening than it should be.

I hear my phone vibrate on my nightstand, and I walk into the room to pick up. I recognize the number on the caller ID, and when I walk back into the hall so I don't wake Julie by answering, the fire's gone, again, not leaving a trace.

"Hey, Erik."

"Alex. It's been a while."

I think about it. "At least four or five years, I guess. Enough that I wasn't sure if Jimmy still... hung out with you."

"Something like that."

I make my way downstairs, trying to keep my voice low enough so that I don't wake anyone. "I'm sure you didn't call me in the middle of the night just to reminisce."

"Yeah. Well I'm all for doing that if you want, but Jimmy told me you might have a bit of a pest problem."

"I guess that's one way of putting it. So... I guess ghosts really do exist?"

"Sure they do. They're a nuisance, like rats. Except they break your stuff instead of pooping on it and biting you."

I think about it. I never really believed in ghosts. If there is something after we die, I like to think it's the heaven Mister Lupino believes in. Not some kind of hell where you get to watch the people you loved go on with their lives and never be able to talk to them or hold them ever again. But I guess Erik would know better than me. "Wow. OK. So... there's nothing broken so far."

"Good. Just disturbances? Jimmy told me a bit."

"Yeah." I take a deep breath. "Just seeing and hearing weird stuff. You know, crying, at night. A weird kid that I know isn't really here. Fire."

"Fire?"

"Yeah."

"Seems like it's something that would be right up your alley."

I sigh. "It's not real fire. It's... ghost fire, I guess. It's not really there. I can tell. Mostly from the not being there three seconds after thing."

"Well, it sounds like a pretty classic haunting."

"Yeah. So... what do I do?"

I hear some shuffling on the other end of the line, like he's looking through paper or something. It lasts a few seconds, and then he sounds triumphant. "Got it."

"Got what?"

"What you need. There's a woman I know. Her name is Agatha Demetriou. She's a medium, and somewhat of a necromancer. Runs in her family. She's exactly what you need. If you've got a ghost, she can find it, and take care of it. I'll give you her number. When you call her, just tell her I sent you, and you shouldn't have a problem."

APRIL 29TH, 1:17 PM

Julie's asleep on the couch when I get in, and I almost feel like joining her. I couldn't get back to sleep last night, and I probably wouldn't have stayed at work even if I hadn't had an appointment to get to. I can hardly keep my eyes open, even if Karen made her coffee extra strong this morning. It's weird, I never felt this tired when I was younger, and it's not like I'm that old yet. Is it?

I sit next to her, and she stirs, looking up at me and flashing me a tired grin when she recognizes me. She shifts so that her head is lying in my lap, sighing softly.

"Hey," I say, settling more comfortably in the couch.

"Hey, handsome. Is it late?"

She glances out the window, and I shake my head. "It's just after lunch." I'm a little worried about where Nicolas is, and I want to ask her, but sitting with her reminds me of the time right before all this started, when it was just me and her at the condo, doing our jobs, not risking our lives, not having loved ones hurting or dying, being able to sit down and watch TV and not think about too many things. I hadn't realized until this moment how things had changed, how crazy and restless life was right now, and it makes me miss those times dearly.

She smiles at me for a long time, and then rolls over to her side so she can wrap her arms loosely around my waist. Her body feels warm in my lap, and I reach over to trail my fingers on her thigh.

"Have you managed to talk to Dow about the situation?" She asks before I manage to touch her.

I let my hand drop, all desire and comfort of the illusion gone as the stress of the past few weeks swarms me again. "No. I waited for him today but he didn't come in."

"Oh." She frowns. "That's unusual, isn't it?"

I shrug. "Well, he's been dealing with a lot of stuff at work lately. I'm sure he was just in court." I don't want to tell her exactly how serious the stuff he's been dealing with is, because then she'd feel even crappier about being stuck at home with the kid, and I hope she doesn't make a big deal out of it. She frowns, but then just shrugs and sits up. The moment's gone and the tension is back, so I just give in to my worry and ask.

"Where's Nicolas?"

"He's out in the yard with your dad, I think."

"Thanks."

I stand, giving her one last glance before walking to the door leading to the small yard. They're both there, just like she said, sitting side by side on a stone bench, looking like they're lost in conversation. They seem to be having a good time, Nicolas is smiling and everything. Mister Lupino has a blanket wrapped around him, and though it hides how skinny and fragile he's become, it doesn't hide all the gear he's connected to.

I watch them for a little while before stepping out to join them. They both hear the door and turn toward me, and I see, for

84

the very first time, a real smile on Nicolas's face, directed at me. I almost stop, and find myself grinning back. Mister Lupino pats my forearm when I reach them.

"Alex, my boy, it is good to see you looking so happy."

"You too, papa." I turn to Nicolas. "You guys having fun?"

Nicolas nods. "He's telling me stories. I don't know if they're true, but they're pretty cool. Are you really a superhero?"

I raise my eyebrows at Mister Lupino, and he just shrugs, but I see that mischievous twinkle in his eye, and shake my head. "Well, I wouldn't put it that way."

"But he said you saved some people. So that wasn't true?"

"Well..." I scratch my head. I never considered myself a hero, much less a superhero. "I did save Mister Lupino's life."

"More than once," Lupino says. "And many more than just mine."

I open my mouth to protest, but I guess maybe he's right. Strictly speaking, I did help get a few people out of rough situations. Lupino. The kids. Luke. Julie. Tom. I never really felt like a hero, though.

"Maybe. That doesn't make me a hero, and certainly not a superhero. I was just there at the right time a lot and did what was necessary."

Mister Lupino's smile widens. "And that is the definition of a hero. They do hard things because no one else can or will do them, and people's lives are better for it."

Nicolas nods, looking serious. "Yeah! Lots of superheroes are like that. Like Spiderman."

I smile. "So I'm Spiderman now?"

He seems to think about it. "Well, obviously you're not Spiderman. 'Cause he's a spider. And he doesn't do fire like you. Do you wear a costume?"

That one makes me laugh wholeheartedly. "No, I don't. Sorry."

"Oh well. It still counts, I guess." He nods to himself, twice, like he's deciding something. "You're a superhero. Is Julie a superhero too?"

I can't help but laugh. "Yeah, she definitely is."

"Cool! Did she save some people?"

"Why don't you go ask her?"

He hops down from his seat. "Ok! See you later, *nonno*!"

He runs to the house. I watch him go, and notice the way that Mister Lupino is smiling at me, with a twinkle of pride in his eye. I sit next to him.

"*Nonno*?"

His smile widens. "You are my son, Alex, if not in name, then definitely in spirit. I had lost hope to ever see your boy again, when you gave him up. To have this chance at being a grandfather again... thank you."

"I'm glad. I'm also glad you're getting along with him, even better than I am. All the superhero talk must help."

He smiles. "It is easier, as a grandparent, to get along with a child. I do not have the responsibility, after all. And Alex, I did mean every word I said. You were a remarkable boy, and you grew up to be a remarkable man."

"Well, I do have some unusual abilities. That doesn't make me a hero, you know." I notice he's staring at me, and I nudge his arm, as gently as I can manage. "I just think you're getting sentimental."

He chuckles softly. "I have always thought you a hero, Alex, my boy. Ever since I met you, and even before, when I heard what you did and were still doing for those children. I am only sorry I did not tell you sooner."

I shake my head, but I'm still smiling. "I think you've always been sentimental."

APRIL 29TH, 3:16 PM

I open the door, and I'm a little surprised at what I see. It's a young girl, looking like she's in her late teens, with dyed purple hair, an 80s style leather jacket over a t-shirt of a band I don't know, and knee high Doc Marten boots. I frown at her, thinking she's come to the wrong address, but she gives me a nod.

"You Alex Lupino?"

"Uh... yeah. You are?"

"My name's Chandra. I'm your medium. Let's see what we have."

I let her in, but frown at her. "I thought Ms. Demetriou..."

"She's my grandmother," the girl says, looking around, not taking her boots off. "Don't worry, I'm as good as she is. It runs in the family, talking to ghosts. She sent me, she's really old and doesn't go out anymore. Plus, I didn't want her visiting a potential psycho."

"Uh... what?"

"She said it was a vampire who gave you her phone number. Only a psycho or an idiot would hang out with a vampire."

I think about that. Jimmy's definitely not an idiot. I guess the psycho part is fair. "I don't hang out with him. We had some business a few years ago, and he... knows one of my best friends."

She purses her lips, and nods once. "All right, if you say so. So, you've got a ghost?"

"I think so. I've been hearing and seeing weird things."

She walks further inside the house, looking at the walls, the ceilings, up the stairs. "You live here alone?"

"No. My father's upstairs, and my girlfriend and my son are gone shopping."

"Good. The less people here, the better. Have they all been seeing the same things as you?"

I frown. I didn't really think to ask. "I don't know. It's happened mostly when I was alone, there was never really an occasion to check with them."

She raises a pierced eyebrow at me. "You'll ask your vampire friend for help before you talk to your family about it?"

"...I guess."

"Weird. All right, let's see what we've got."

She starts walking all over the house, letting her hands hover over walls, furniture, objects. She frowns once or twice, but doesn't really stop or say anything throughout the whole process. I don't interfere either, letting her do her thing, whatever that is, though I do prevent her from going into Lupino's room, because I don't want his nap disturbed.

When she's reached the last room there is to see, she turns to me, shaking her head. "I can't feel anything."

"What does that mean?"

She shrugs. "Could mean it's dormant. Could mean you're a crazy person."

I take a deep breath, trying to remain calm. I never even considered the possibility that I might be crazy, and she's saying it like it's nothing. "So... how do we find out which is which?"

"Find me a nice quiet place. I gotta sit down somewhere so I can concentrate."

I don't say anything, just bring her to the den. She pushes the small coffee table aside, I guess for some room, because she sits down on the floor in front of the TV, legs crossed, her hands on her knees. She closes her eyes and just sits there, quietly, not doing anything. I fold my arms and watch her. It lasts for a while at least ten minutes, and I start pacing up and down the den. Finally she turns to me, and she really doesn't seem very happy.

"Yeah, so... I can't find anything. No trace of a presence."

"What does that mean?"

She stands. "Well, when there is a haunting, no matter the level of activity, there is always at least some kind of residual trace, and you can detect it by concentrating. And with the level of activity you described, it shouldn't be that hard to find. But there's nothing. There hasn't been a spirit here for a very, very long time, if there ever was. I'm sorry."

The way she's speaking, and looking at me... I've seen that look before. It was the look the doctor had when he gave Mister Lupino the verdict. The day that I learned what

91

'metastasize' means. That was a death sentence. This can only mean one thing.

"So... you think it's all in my head. You think I'm crazy."

"Sorry dude. I have no other explanation for you." She takes a pause, like she's letting me digest the news. After a minute or two, she shifts from one foot to the other. "Listen... I'm gonna waive the fee for this time. Anyway, my grandma owed this friend of yours a favor, and... well it's not like I found anything. So... good luck and all that."

She waves awkwardly, and turns around, showing herself out of the house, leaving me alone with what's left of my mind.

APRIL 29TH, 11:49 PM

This is starting to become a bad habit; I'm lying awake in bed again, staring at the ceiling, Julie asleep next to me. It's a few nights now that I've been having trouble sleeping; I hope it'll start getting better as all the changes settle themselves into a new routine. Right now, though, all I can do is try to clear my head, as impossible as that seems. The possibility that I really am losing my mind is a little much to deal with.

I haven't told anyone. I didn't tell Julie what the appointment was about, and I certainly haven't told her the results. If I am losing my mind, I want to make sure that this is what's really going on before I have to discuss it with her. She's pretty understanding, and we're good together, but I don't know if she'd be OK with something like that.

Of course, that's what's running through my mind when I hear the sobbing again. I stay in bed, tossing and turning for what seems like hours, trying to ignore it. If this is really in my head, it should go away if I ignore it, right?

Eventually I get up, just to check to make double sure it isn't Nicolas. As soon as I swing my feet over the edge of the bed and put them on the ground, I know it isn't him, and I regret even sitting up.

It's that little girl again. I try to tell myself it's just my eyes playing tricks on me, and that it's Nicolas, but it's impossible to mistake her for him, even if I still can't make out her face, since she's covering it with her hands. Her shoulders are shaking and jumping up and down, the sobbing obviously coming from her.

I think about it for a long time, but eventually I manage to make up my mind, and reach out a hand to shake Julie awake. She groans, her eyes still closed.

"What is it?"

"Open your eyes. Please."

She blinks up at me, and frowns. "Are you all right?"

I point to the door, where the girl is still standing. "Can you see her?"

She looks at the door, and judging by the look on her face, it's plain what her answer will be. "Who?"

I shake my head. "Never mind."

She frowns at me. "Are you all right, Alex?"

"Yeah. Yeah, I'm fine. Sorry. I thought..." I glance at the door. The girl is still standing there, sobbing so loud I can barely hear myself speak. "It's nothing. Go back to sleep."

Julie seems about to say something, but then she just sighs and lies back down. "Fine. Good night."

I don't answer, just bringing my feet up on the bed again. It seems to take hours for the girl to disappear.

APRIL 30ᵀᴴ, 8:17 AM

Karen is already there when I walk into the office the next day. She looks tired but she's already made some coffee. I couldn't face Julie and the questions she might have about what happened last night. I don't really want to be here, here but I'm already dreading going home. I manage to pass the time until Dow arrives, even though I don't get much done.

He walks right by my office when he gets in, probably not expecting me to be here that early. I have to get up and chase him into the hallway. He stops when he notices me, and blinks at me, surprised.

"Hey Alex, I didn't expect to see you here this early. What's up?"

"A bunch of things. You have any time?"

"Sure, no problem."

I motion for him to follow me to my office, and he does, sitting down. He puts his briefcase on the ground, and frowns up at me.

"If this is about the registry," he says, "I still don't have any news yet."

I frown. "No, it wasn't about that. Although I'd like you to keep me posted with what happens with that. I was wondering if you'd had time to think about what I talked to you about the other day."

He frowns at me, looking confused. "What you talked to me about?"

"You know, about Nicolas. About how he needs someone to look after him, and it can't be Julie?"

"Right." He runs a hand through his hair. I notice that his forehead seems larger than before, and I can see the scalp more on top of his head; I guess he must be starting to go bald. I never noticed before; Mister Lupino is really old, but he still has his hair, only it's white. I never really thought about what mine would turn out like. I was never overly concerned with my appearance, but then I never really thought I'd live to get old. I wonder if I'll go bald too. "I've looked into options. It seems to me that I might have a solution that could take care of both of our problems."

"Oh yeah?"

He nods. "Yeah about the kid that had the little accident at school, you know, with her dream? Well I've been thinking and I think our best bet would be to open a school here."

I frown. "A school? Do we even have the resources for that?"

"Well it wouldn't be a big school. Just a small class that we could grow as we need, to get the kids that have dangerous powers out of the classroom. That way, no one poses a danger to the public and maybe the government would abandon this whole business about the registry."

I raise my eyebrows; I'm actually kind of impressed. "Have you actually found someone to do this?"

He shakes his head. "Not yet; but I have a few people in mind. We need a powerful null who's also qualified as a teacher. There aren't that many around."

I have an unwelcome, fleeting thought of the classroom at GenEx, and being unable to use my powers in the class. The feeling had been unnerving, but I knew for sure none of my classmates could use theirs, either.

"That's actually a really good idea," I say. "Julie's gonna be really happy to hear that. Let me know as soon as you have news."

He nods with a smile, picks up his suitcase, and walks away. I relax into my chair, feeling like things are finally starting to go right. I start looking through the files that Karen has rearranged, trying to make sense of her system. It's brain-numbing work, but it feels good to do, and for the next few hours, my day doesn't get any worse.

I start having that sense of impending doom, the way I do when I feel things go too well, and it doesn't get any better when my phone rings, and I see that it's Julie. I try to ignore the feeling as I pick up.

"Hey, Julie! I have good news! I just spoke to Dow, and – "

"Alex..."

I frown, and instinctively sit back down. She's using her bad-news sort of voice, and she's calling me by my name instead of some term of endearment. Looks like I was right; there's something wrong. I hope it isn't Nicolas.

"...there's something I gotta tell you."

"Then just say it." She doesn't respond, and I take a breath through my nose, trying to cool down. "Sorry. I didn't mean to snap at you. You know I hate it when people beat around the bush."

"I know. It's just... it's Mister Lupino."

That takes the breath out of me just like jumping in a pool that's way too cold. I've been so focused on Nicolas I almost forgot what was happening to Mister Lupino. It can't be; I haven't properly said goodbye, yet.

"Don't worry. He's not dead." I can hear the unspoken 'yet' that goes at the end of her words, but I'm still relieved. I want to take advantage of all the time I have left, and I really haven't been, lately. "He's taken a turn for the worst, though. He... the nurse said there wasn't much time left. I think you should come home as soon as you can."

"OK."

I let the call end with her hanging up, and I stare at my phone for a few seconds before I can make myself stand. I just walk away, in a sort of daze, and when I walk out I come face to face with Karen in the hall. She frowns at me.

"Mister Lupino? Is everything all right?"

"No. I'm going home. Hold my calls. Tell them I won't be back for a while. Call me on my cell phone if there's anything. I probably won't answer, though, so don't do that unless it's urgent."

She mumbles something, but it doesn't register.

APRIL 30ᵀᴴ, 9:29 PM

Hearing his raspy, struggling breath is almost a relief: it's so slow, and it comes at such long intervals, that it happens pretty often that I wonder if he's gone already. When I got home, and found everyone gathered in the living room, Rosanna, Jeanine, the nurse, Julie, and Nicolas, and found out he had slipped into a coma, I hated myself. I should have been there, with him, spent as much time as I could by his side, taken advantage of the time I could still speak to him. Now, I may never get another chance. It's not fair to him that I abandoned him. I didn't need to be away. How could I delude myself into thinking I needed a break from home?

I can't stop thinking about Nicolas. When I saw him, I could see he'd been crying, but he wouldn't tell me what was wrong. Julie told me that she had it under control, and I mean I trust her, of course, but... It really doesn't help to know that my son would rather turn to her than me for support. I know he and Lupino had gotten to know each other well, and that he was getting attached to the old man. This is probably a blow to him, and once again, I can do nothing to prevent it from happening.

It looks like I can do nothing for anyone else, either. Not even me. These are my last hours with Lupino. With the man who meant the most to me in my life. The one whose example I use every day, to wonder what kind of man I want to be. And all I can do, now, is hold his cold, unresponsive hand, and watch the shell of the giant he used to be struggle for breath, through eyes not quite closed, his head at an odd backward angle which lets his slack jaw fall forward, giving his open mouth an odd look. The nurse said he would probably never wake again, that he would be gone during the night, or tomorrow at the most. They left the machines monitoring him on, but the IV is gone.

There are so many things I want to tell him. So many things I want him to know. Sometimes, I'm moved to say them out loud, thinking, deep down, somewhere, that he can hear me, but even at those times, I can't find the right words, and I just babble incoherently about wishing we had more time. More often than not, though, there are just no words, no thoughts, nothing adequate to this moment.

The worst part is, I'm starting to doze off. Karen made me a whole pot of coffee at work, and Julie made me some more, earlier, after she put Nicolas to sleep, but that's all gone. It's weird that I should be falling asleep with how stressed I am, but my stupid eyes keep closing on their own. I let go of his hand to rub my face vigorously, trying to keep awake, but I still feel groggy after this.

The door opens slowly, and Julie pokes her head in. When she sees that I'm awake, she comes in all the way, carrying a tray on which is a bowl of steaming soup, some bread and a glass of water. I stand to go meet her.

"Did I miss dinner? Sorry."

She smiles and whispers. "Don't worry about it. Has he...?"

I look back at Mister Lupino, who's lying on his back, completely still, his ragged breath coming through his open mouth.

"No. There's no change. How's Nicolas?"

She shrugs and puts the tray on the tall dresser near the door. "He's OK. He's adjusting, I think. Poor kid."

I run my hand over my hair. "Maybe I should..." Before I'm done, I hear a shrill scream coming from the hallway, followed by the unmistakable, terrified sobs of a child. In my state of confusion and preoccupation, I run out of the room, and I'm out in the hall long before I remember about the maybe-ghost.

Julie runs after me, and I stop in the middle of the hall, looking at her. She looks surprised, and takes a step back. "Alex, what's wrong?"

As if I really needed the confirmation that it wasn't really Nicolas crying, I see him on a stool in the bathroom, in his pajamas, toothbrush in hand, frothy toothpaste around his mouth. The sobs keep getting louder, but obviously, they're not coming from him. He frowns at me when he notices that I'm staring.

Julie grabs my forearm and turns me around; I can see the worry tinged with a bit of anger in her eyes. "What is wrong with you, Alex?"

"Don't you hear that?"

"Hear what?"

"The girl! She's crying! Tell me you can hear it too!"

Her eyes are wide with alarm, and I see that I am gripping her shoulders, though I don't remember moving my hands. She stares at me, fear and worry so obvious in her eyes that I can't stand it anymore, and I look away. She opens her mouth and speaks, but the sobs are so loud I'm having a hard time understanding what she's saying; there's no way that I'm having a conversation under these circumstances. Not wanting to scare my son any more than I already have, I just walk back out of his line of sight, hoping she'll have the good sense to go take care of him.

She doesn't. She runs after me. "Alex! What is it?"

"Nothing!" I'm snapping at her, but it's hard not to do with that horrible sound filling my head. What's wrong with me? "Just get him to bed. I'm gonna go eat."

I don't give her time to respond before I walk into Mister Lupino's room, shutting the door behind me. He's still exactly where I left him. How could he sleep with all that noise?

He probably doesn't hear it. Just like everyone else, it seems.

APRIL 30TH, 11:43 PM

She seems asleep by the time I walk in, so I creep in as quietly as I can, taking off my pants before I go sit on the edge of the bed. As soon as I do, I feel her shifting, and she sits up, turning on her bedside lamp. I look at her, hesitantly, over my shoulder, and it's as I feared: she looks concerned, like I'm about to bite her head off.

"Hey," she says, as if there's nothing wrong, though her face is telling me a different story.

"Hey."

"Alex... are you OK?"

I sigh and lean my head in my hands. "I don't know."

She crawls up to me, and wraps her arms around my waist, leaning her head on my back. The familiar gesture comforts me a bit, but not enough.

"Are you seeing things?"

I let out a long breath, feeling my body sag. "...I guess I am." I thought it would feel better to admit it, but it doesn't. Now it just makes me feel anxious to know what she's going to think.

She brushes my hair out of the way and kisses the back of my neck. "You've been under so much stress," she says softly. "And you haven't been sleeping well lately. It's probably just that."

I feel my shoulders relaxing, relief washing over me like warm water. "Yeah. It's probably just that. It'll probably get better when I get some sleep."

She leans her head on my shoulder, peering at me over it. "Just to make sure, though... Maybe you should see a doctor? You know, someone who can make sure that it's really just you being tired?"

I frown. I've never really trusted head doctors. After I first ran off, when I was twelve, and the man my mother made me with broke my arm, they sent me to a head doctor, who asked me a bunch of questions and then decided I had an 'anger issue', and that's what made them decide to make me stay in that shithole of a 'family home'; it wasn't that man's fault that he was getting drunk and beating the crap out of me, he was just 'reacting to my anger'.

"I dunno, Julie. I'll think about it."

She sighs heavily, pressing her forehead against my shoulder. I think she's going to argue, for a moment, but she doesn't. "All right. Sounds good. Now come to bed. Time for you to get that rest."

MAY 1ˢᵀ, 8:17 AM

I can hear Julie laughing at something Nicolas said. I think about waiting for them to be done with breakfast before I go down, but I don't know whether or not they're leaving, so I might as well just go.

I don't bother with getting dressed, just drag myself downstairs wearing only my boxers and a t-shirt. I glance at Mister Lupino's room as I pass it, but I can't make myself go in just yet.

Rosanna is sitting with Julie and Nicolas at the table, when I get to the dining room. She gets up when she sees me, coming to kiss my cheek.

"Alex! Let me serve you breakfast. Would you like some biscuits?"

I make myself smile. "No, thanks, Rosanna. I'll just have some coffee, please."

She gives me a look like she's about to scold me, but doesn't argue. I'm not sure if I should be worried about this or not, but I'm so tired and empty that I can barely think about it.

When I sit at the table, I notice that Julie and Nicolas are both eyeing me warily. It's a lot more obvious on Nicolas's face, but I know Julie well enough that the slight tension in her smile speaks volumes. I wish I could wonder what's wrong with them, but I know. They think I'm going nuts. I can't even disagree.

"Did you sleep well?" Julie gives me an obviously fake smile as she takes a bite in her biscuit. I sigh; there's no point in lying, especially if I look half as bad as I feel.

"Not really."

"Hmm. Well, maybe you should take the day off. Rest up a bit. Hey, you could help us paint Nicolas's room! We've decided on a *Star Wars* theme."

"Oh!" I try to look happy for him. "That sounds good. So you like *Star Wars*?"

He nods, and at least, he seems genuinely enthusiastic. "Yes! C-3P0 and R2D2 are the best."

"They sure are." I try to sound like I know what I'm talking about. "Well, maybe we can buy you plushies of them, and decorations, too."

He rolls his eyes; I guess I missed the mark. "They're robots. They don't make plushies of robots, they make robots!"

For whatever reason, his exasperation with me is making me feel a bit better; I find it in me to really smile at Rosanna when she puts my coffee down in front of me. "Sorry, buddy. I guess you'll have to teach me."

He smiles, a bit shyly. "Maybe you could come with us when we go shopping?"

I lick my lips. I want nothing more than to say 'of course, I will,' but at the same time... I don't know if I should leave Mister Lupino alone. What if something happens while I'm gone?

Julie shakes her head; she's always been pretty good at reading my mind, even if I she can't actually literally do that. "Sorry sweetie, he has to stay here today. His daddy is very sick and needs him." She flashes me a smile that's full of pity, and I have to look away. Even with her, after everything, I can't bear to see that expression. "Don't worry about it," she says. "I'll go, and we'll be back in no time. You take care of things here."

"Alex. Wake up, my boy. I must speak with you."

I look up, rubbing my face, and see Mister Lupino sitting up in bed, looking down at me seriously. I blink. "Papa! You're feeling better!"

He smiles kindly, but doesn't answer. Instead, he just puts his hand on my shoulder. "We must speak, my son. I'm afraid we do not have much time."

I frown. What does he mean? I find myself nodding. "Um… sure. What do you need to talk about?"

"You. I need to tell you what a fine man you have become."

I shrug, and look away. He might be saying this, but…

"I mean it, my son. You have made me more proud than you can ever know. But I need you to know this. You have grown into a kind, generous, responsible, strong man. You have nothing to fear, and nothing to worry about for yourself, or your family, except for one very important thing."

Why is he telling me this? What is he getting at? I have so many questions, I'm not sure what to ask, so I go for what seems the most obvious. "What? What thing?"

"Your son. He needs his father. Desperately. I know that this is not an easy time for you but it is not for him, either. And he needs you. You need him, as well. Find solace in each other. Do not let him suffer alone."

I frown, and stare at him. He hasn't spent that much time with Nicolas. Could they have gotten this close already? How does he know how my relationship with him is going?

"I just... thought I would give him his space... and besides... he has enough to deal with right now without knowing..."

"He needs you. He just does not know how to express it. He is, after all, his father's son."

I frown at him. "But... I mean... how do I know? How do you know, for that matter? He needs someone better than me. Julie's better than me."

"She is not his mother. He has no one left in the world, but you. You need to be there for him. Remember, you pushed me away when we first met. You did not think you could give me anything of value. But you did. And we are both better men for having known each other. Do not deprive your son of this, and do not deprive yourself of your son. You need to take advantage of this time. It is limited, and goes by far faster than you would imagine."

I sigh, and run both my hands over my hair. Why do I feel so panicky? So stressed out? What's wrong with me? It's like I'm falling off a cliff. "But what if I screw him up even further? What if I..."

He gives me a light shake, which helps me focus again. I look at him. He's looking at me seriously, with an air of believing what he says is terribly important, which I suppose it is.

"Alex. Think about it. I did not always consider myself the best father. I lost one son, to terrible circumstances, which I always believed I could and should have prevented. Do not make the mistake I did, of holding back too much. Live your life with your son. Be there for him. The one thing you could do that would, as you put it, screw him up... would be to abandon him in his time of need. He needs you to be there, to feel like the entire world has not turned his back on him."

I stare at him. I suppose he's right. Nicolas's adoptive father has turned his back on him. So has his mother, in a way, and he probably feels responsible for all of that. I know I did, when it happened to me. And I know what it's like thinking that the world would be a much better place if you just died. I can't let him think that. It's not true, and he doesn't deserve it.

"Thank you so much, papa. For everything."

As I say the words, I realize I mean exactly what they say. It's not just the advice. Or the way he's pointing me what to do. It's taking me in. Letting me share his life. Trusting me. Showing me that I had worth, no matter what I'd been through, no matter what I'd done. Giving me a chance. He lets all of that sink in, like he knows what I'm thinking, and then he just smiles, and nods, kindly, and I wake up.

I'm half sitting on the chair, with my head in my arms, which are folded across his legs.

He's lying there, not moving, as usual, and I realize I must have been dreaming, though it didn't really feel like a dream. When he was sitting, he looked healthy, not so thin and yellow, like he is now, but strong, like he was a few years ago, when

111

we traveled to Italy together. Now, though, he's just lying there and... what is that sound? It sounds like the heart monitor's beep, except it's like the button's stuck. I look up, and when I see it, I understand, and I don't at the same time. The line is flat. All the lines are flat. Nothing is moving. He's not breathing. His heart has stopped. He's dead. He's gone.

I stand up, taking a step back, and stumble when I get my feet caught in the chair. I keep staring at him, but I don't really see him. It's not even him anymore. It's just a body. Did his heart stopping make that change, or did he stop being the man I knew when he slipped into this coma? When he lost all that weight? When he couldn't talk anymore? Or walk? Or go to the bathroom by himself? I can't breathe. My chest and throat both feel tight, my eyes, sting, and my heart is beating so hard, and so fast, that I think every vein in my body might burst.

I have no idea how long I'm standing there for, just staring at him, or at what used to be him, but at some point, I realize that my cheeks are wet, and that I'm gasping for breath, and I reach for the chair, feeling like the floor is disappearing from under me. I don't find it, because I kicked it over when I stood, so I just sink, until my butt hits the floor, staring at the bed. I always heard that when you die, your life flashes before your eyes; but I'm not dying, and I keep seeing memories of times I had with him, the dinners, the chess games, him playing with my son, coaxing me to read, to learn Italian... it's over. He's over. He's gone.

Dimly, I hear footsteps coming up the stairs, over the annoying sound of the heart monitor, and I try wiping my eyes, though I do it halfheartedly. I don't really care who sees what right now. Lupino's gone. He's *gone*. Rosanna appears in the doorway, and I hear a strangled moan escape her throat as she pauses, and then rushes to the bed to take Lupino's hand. She starts moaning and crying and talking in Italian, and though I now speak it fluently, I don't understand what she says. She could be speaking Chinese, or English, and it wouldn't matter; I don't feel like anything's ever going to make sense again, now that he's no longer here. Her grief is loud, and strong, and reverberates off the walls, into the hall, and possibly the whole neighborhood; mine is silent, and speechless, but it feels like I'm containing a thousand nuclear bombs, inside, and if I let out one peep, one tiny bit of it, the sheer force of it will rush out of me and flatten half the country. I start feeling numb, little by little. It starts in my chest, and spreads to my arms, my fingers, my legs, my face. I feel like I couldn't move a muscle if I tried, and I don't, because I'm afraid that I could do it, that I could actually pick myself up and walk out of here and the world would go on, like it has any right to.

Eventually, Rosanna lets go of his hand, and turns to kneel next to me, squeezing me in her arms tight enough to hurt, and I'm glad I'm so numb, because if her grief and mine could connect, then it would go on forever, until all of it, all the life, all the blood and feeling would pour out of us and nothing would be left.

MAY 1ST, 6:34 PM

The coffee's cold in my cup. I've taken a sip or two, but it feels like my throat is way too tight to swallow anything. I've been sitting in the kitchen for a while, talking with Rosanna, or listening to her talk about Mister Lupino. I still feel numb. Rosanna called the nurse, who came, and called the coroner, who came and went, taking... what remained. Now Rosanna's gone, and the house is starting to get dark, and I just sit there, with the cup of coffee she made me when we came downstairs. I still don't know how to feel, or what to say. I feel like anything I do just means that life goes on, and that's as insulting as it is absurd.

The front door opens and shuts, and I finally find the courage to make myself put the cup down on the counter. I want to get up, and switch on the light, but the thought doesn't make it to my muscles. I hear Julie call out, and I can't even make myself answer her. I haven't said anything since it happened. I think I forgot how to make my voice work.

"Alex! We're home! Alex?" I hear footsteps going up the stairs, and the rustle of plastic bags being put down. The steps come back down, a lot more frantic, and she calls out again. "Alex?"

I find my voice, though it's cracked and weak. "I'm in the kitchen."

I hear a few people coming, but she makes it first. She takes one look at my face, and being who she is, she understands right away. She walks over to hold me in her arms, lightly, and it makes me feel better. I think it's because she wants to give me the comfort she thinks I need, unlike Rosanna, who just wanted to squeeze something to ease and share her own pain.

"I'm so sorry, Alex."

The words are simple, and cliché, and expected, but the way she says them, and because they come from her, at that moment, they make the air go out of the room all over again, and my lungs collapse on themselves. My arms twitch up, wanting to hold her, and my throat is tight and my eyes sting, but I can't make myself do it; I've seen Nicolas walk in. I can't cry in front of him. I can't let him see me this way. He needs me to make the world OK, for him, and for the first time, it does feel like it might be OK that the world keeps going. I push Julie away, slightly, and she looks down at me, concerned, but then she sees me looking at Nicolas, and I think she understands, because she doesn't push the issue.

She goes to him. "Nicolas... I think we better..."

I shake my head, interrupting. "No. It's OK. I'm OK. Come here, Nicolas. Come tell me about your day."

He frowns at me like he's not sure, and then looks at Julie. She doesn't acknowledge the gesture, making it obvious that I'm the one who should tell Nicolas what to do, not her. Nicolas seems to accept this, and walks towards me. I pull up a seat, and he climbs on it, hesitantly.

"Is *Nonno* still sleeping?"

For a few moments, I'm completely unable to draw breath; I exchange a look with Julie. I need to tell him at some point, but for now, it seems like too much to deal with, both for me and for him.

"He's gone. A doctor took him away, to... look after him."

I'm not lying, exactly; the coroner is a kind of doctor, isn't he? Nicolas frowns, looking at my face like he's searching it for the truth, but after a few seconds he seems to accept what I'm saying. I'm not sure enough, though, so I just go ahead and change the subject.

"So, did you find some nice decorations for your room?"

He nods, smiling. "We got some posters, and some paint, and Julie said she knew someone who was real good at drawing, and painting and stuff, and she's gonna draw me a big R2D2 for the wall, and a frame of him with C3P0, and there's gonna be light-sabers, and..."

I lean my head in my hand, listening to him talk about a bunch of things I know nothing about, and it doesn't matter, because he's so excited, he's grinning, and making gestures with his hands. His eyes are a dark sort of blue, darker than mine, and they sort of curve at the bottom when he smiles. There's a funny little gap between his two front teeth, and a dimple in both his cheeks. I was so worried about everything that I never took the time to really watch him, and he truly looks wonderful, probably the cutest kid in the world.

It feels so absurdly good to see him be happy right now, like the last few hours didn't really happen, and are nothing but a distant memory. Even better, Julie stops watching me like I'm suddenly going to explode or something, and she goes about putting whatever it is they bought away. She also bought a bucket of chicken, which she quietly brings to the kitchen, and serves us. The meal is eaten in relative silence, except for Nicolas talking about *Star Wars*, and there's no mention of the cold coffee on the table, or the empty bed upstairs. By the time we put Nicolas to bed, I'm feeling like life might really go on after this.

117

Julie is awkward with me afterward, obviously wanting to talk, but not actually saying anything. She stays silent, inhaling once or twice as if getting ready to say something, but changing her mind at the last minute. Once we're in bed, there are a few lingering looks that remind me how I'm supposed to be feeling, and there is a long embrace that makes my throat tight again, but she lets go and turns off the light when I don't return it.

I lie awake in bed for hours, just listening to Julie breathe, and I don't know if it's that sound, or the fact that I'm thinking about my son right now, but I don't see or hear anything out of the ordinary that night.

MAY 2ND, 8:39 AM

I finally make my way down the stairs and into the living room. I must've spent a good hour standing in front of Mister Lupino's door, just staring at it, unable to move, thinking if I don't open the door, maybe everything that happened yesterday didn't really happen and he's still there.

I turn on the TV and start flipping through the channels, just to have something to take my mind off things. I could probably make some coffee, but I feel like I just don't have the energy. Rosanna is not coming in today; she was supposed to, and she said she didn't mind, but I gave her the day off. I think out of everybody, she was probably one of the three people who loved Mister Lupino the most.

I hear steps in the stairs, and when I turn my head to see who's coming, it's Nicolas. He's wearing his pajamas, and is holding both his stuffed pig, which Julie retrieved from the office, and the stuffed bunny that used to be his and I gave him back. He comes to stand next to me, frowning at me. I do my best to give him a convincing smile.

"Hey buddy," I say. "You hungry? I have no idea what we have but we could go find out."

119

He shakes his head. "I'm not hungry. Where's *Nonno*?"

I sigh. "He's not here."

"When is he coming back?"

I put down the remote control, feeling suddenly extremely tired. "I dunno."

He frowns at me seriously. "He's not coming back, is he?"

I lean forward, propping my elbows against my knees. I take a deep breath. "No. I'm sorry."

He sits down next to me, cautiously, on the edge of the couch, like he's hoping to make a quick getaway soon. "Is he… dead?"

I lift my hand to put it on his shoulder, but then put it down again. I've never really touched him in a comforting manner, or really at all, and I'm generally bad with that stuff. I am good at being straightforward, though, and he is my son, so he's gotta be a little bit like me, right?

"Yeah. He is. Do you know what that means?"

He frowns, and nods, bringing his feet up on the couch and hugging his knees. He doesn't say anything, and I have no idea what to say. We stay silent for a little while, until I get uncomfortable enough to fill the silence.

"I'm so sorry, buddy. You know…"

"I want my mommy."

"Sorry?"

He looks at me, and I can see his eyes are full of tears. His voice quivers when he repeats. "I want my mommy! I want to go home! I don't want to be here anymore!"

I lift my hand again, this time with the firm intention of comforting him. "Look, Nicolas..."

He slaps my hand away, shouting. "You're not my daddy! *Nonno* was the only person who liked me here, and now he's dead! I want to go home! I want to be with my mom and dad! I don't want to be here anymore!"

I take a deep breath, trying to stay calm, to not let the hurt come out as anger like it always does. "I'm sorry. I know this isn't easy, but... you can't. You can't go back there."

"Yes I can!" He stands up from the couch, as if his sitting position can't contain his anger anymore. I feel the hair stand up on my arms; there's a feeling of energy radiating from him. "You can't make me stay here," he continues. "I want my mommy! I hate you!"

As he screams that last sentence, there's a sudden burst of electric sound from the television, and it goes dark. I could swear I can still hear a slight frying sound coming from it. I turn to Nicolas, and I don't know what he sees in my eyes, because he just drops to the floor and starts crying. I stare at him for a few seconds, unsure of what to do, and I slide down to the couch to bring myself to his level. I reach out to hug him, and he screams.

"Don't touch me! Get away from me! I'll hurt you too! I hurt everyone!"

I hear someone running down the stairs, and I look up to see Julie hurrying toward us. I stand, relieved, as she bursts into the living room.

121

She stops, looking down at Nicolas, and then at me. She's breathless, and looks a little frazzled. "What happened?"

"We were talking about..." I take a deep breath. I don't know what else could happen if I say anything. "He got upset. And... the TV."

She takes a look at the TV, from which a tiny tendril of smoke is escaping. She frowns at it, and then bends down and touches Nicolas's forearm gently, probably taking away his power. He lets her touch him, hiccupping and leaning into her.

"I d-didn't m-mean to!" He sobs. "It w-was an accident!"

She wraps her arms around him; he looks so tiny by comparison to her. He starts sobbing in earnest then, and she strokes his hair. She seems at ease with him, a lot more than I've seen her be in the beginning; I guess it could be all the time they've spent together lately, but I can't help but feel inadequate. He would never let me get this close, and I'm actually his father.

I leave her to her comforting, and walk out. I don't care that I'm just wearing jeans and a t-shirt, or that I haven't showered or shaved. I need to be away from here.

MAY 3RD, 11:37 AM

I've been staring at the same file for over an hour. I've had four cups of coffee already, so I know this isn't just about being tired; I guess there's too much on my mind for me to concentrate on work right now.

I've been wanting to talk to Dow, not even really about work, but maybe about what happened, about anything, really, but he's been in court all morning again, about this stupid registry thing. I hope it doesn't go through. Really, it should have me a lot more nervous than I am, but it's like my head is so full of worrying about other things that it barely registers on my radar.

I keep stealing glances at the door, hoping to catch him when he comes back, when he does get here, he ducks into my office, knocking lightly on the open door. I put down the file gratefully and motion for him to come inside. He sits down, watching me.

"Hey, Alex. How are you holding up?"

For half a second, I don't know what he's talking about, but of course, his mother must have told him. She and Mister Lupino had been dating. Thinking of him takes the wind out of my lungs, and all I can think of for a moment is that he's gone, he won't give me any more advice, he won't make fun of the way I play chess,

I won't ever see him smile ever again. I'm dizzy, to the extent that I almost fall off my chair, and it probably takes me at least a minute to regain my composure. When I do, I shrug, hoping I'm dismissive enough, but harboring no delusions of success. "I'm OK."

He purses his lips, but doesn't say anything about my obvious shift in mood. Instead, he leans forward, propping his elbows on the desk. "When is the funeral?"

"Saturday, at eleven."

"Do you need anything?"

I shake my head. "He... he arranged everything when he learned..." I lick my lips, and take a deep breath. It feels like trying not to break down has been all I've been doing lately. "It's all set." He nods, and opens his mouth, probably to talk more about it, like there's any need for that. I speak before he can say anything. "Anyway, what I really wanted to ask you... Have you found anyone for that school thing you were talking about?"

He frowns, and for a few seconds I think he's going to insist on talking about Mister Lupino, but he sighs, and runs his hand over his coat lapel, smoothing it, leaning back in his chair. "Not yet. But, if Julie's having a hard time, I can talk to her. Maybe my wife could take the kid off your hands for a little while."

I sigh. "I don't think so. This morning... he got upset, and he broke the TV."

"Broke the TV?"

"Well, sort of. As he got more and more upset, it just... I guess something exploded inside. It made that weird fizzing noise and then there was smoke coming out of it."

"And you're sure it was him?"

"I guess it could have been a coincidence," I admit. "But from how guilty he looked, I don't think so."

"What made him upset?" I give him a sideways look, and he understands. "Oh," he says. "I didn't realize they were... close."

"They got along well. I think it's kind of the straw that broke the camel's back, you know? After he found out, he asked me to take him back to his adoptive mom and dad."

"What did you tell him?"

"Well, the truth! That I couldn't bring him there."

"The whole truth?"

I sigh. Why is everyone pressuring me to have a big emotional discussion with him? "Just that I couldn't bring him back there. That's it. It was enough, and even if I had wanted to continue down that train of thought, well the TV exploded. It was a little distracting."

"Hmm." He purses his lip, and looks down. I know he's going to say something to disagree with me now; he never makes that sound when he's satisfied. "And you think that finding a teacher will resolve the situation?"

"Yeah!" I frown at him. He's insinuating something, and I don't know what it is, so it bugs me even more than it usually would. "Being with a null, he wouldn't be able to break anything, or hurt anybody, and he could learn to control it."

Dow raises an eyebrow at me. "You really think that this is how he's going to learn to control his ability?"

"That's what teachers are for, right? Teaching?"

"Certain things, I suppose." He gives me a sad sort of look. "But you know... this isn't a permanent solution. I mean, what happens if he wants to go somewhere for a sleepover? Or when he grows up and wants to have a girlfriend? Are you going to hire a null to follow him around for the rest of his life?"

I frown. He's got a point, but I don't really want him to be right. "Well... it could get better as he gets older. It's how it was with me. I got older, and I got it under control."

"Maybe. But you may want to think about another solution." He picks up his things and stands. "Anyway, I have to get back to work." He looks up at me, and I guess I must look like crap, because he sighs and gives me a fake smile. "Don't worry. I'll try to think of something too."

MAY 3ᴿᴰ, 6:13 PM

I can hear Julie and Nicolas talking from the second floor when I get in, so I start up the stairs to go see them. I still haven't really figured what I'm going to tell him, about his power, about his actual relationship to me, about anything. Maybe I'll figure it out by the time that I get there, but I doubt it.

I try not to look at Mister Lupino's room when I pass in front of it, and since Julie closed the door, it's a little easier. But even though it's closed, the door seems so painfully obvious there, that it seems to lurk, to fill the hall with its malevolent presence, to want to get in my mind and obliterate everything else.

As I reach the second floor, there's something weird about it. It still looks extremely familiar, but it's not the second floor of Mister Lupino's house. The walls are covered in pastel floral wallpaper that I know I've seen before, but definitely not here. Maybe at Erik's ugly house? It's stained and ripped in some places. There're also only walls where doors should be. I look around, confused, wondering what the hell is going on now.

As I'm standing, I hear a low sort of rumble. It's not a rumble, exactly, it's like water rushing, but quieter. I turn to face the direction, and it seems to me the hall is getting darker.

I squint, and turn around to see if it's just me, but before I have time to properly wonder about it, the place gets really bright, and I see a wall of fire coming my way. Instinctively, I brace myself, and try to nullify the fire with my power, snuff it, anything, but it doesn't react to me at all; it just keeps unfurling toward me, bright and huge and hot, so hot. I have time to wonder that I'm feeling heat before I have to put up my arms and scream like any ordinary person, protecting my face, feeling my skin boil and burn and peel and crack. I've never felt that before; I've never been burnt. It's so much more painful than I thought it would be, I'm sure I'm gonna pass out.

I lie writhing and screaming on the floor, in agony, when I suddenly feel a hand on my shoulder, and I hear Julie's soothing voice. Suddenly the pain is gone, like it never existed. I stop screaming, gasp, and look at my arms: nothing. I feel my face, my hair, but it all feels normal, like I'm fine, like none of this happened. Julie is frowning at me, concerned.

"Alex? What happened? Are you all right?"

I want to answer her, but I don't even know where to begin, so I just stare, dumb, my mouth hanging open, with nothing to say. I remember how I wasn't able to put out the fire, and my stomach clenches; I try to tell myself that this isn't the first time, that there was the time in the dining room too, where I saw fire and I couldn't stop it, and I try to tell myself that it's not my power, it's just all in my head, but I can't help it. In my panic, I open my hands, making flames, and finally feel at least a tiny bit of relief. At least there's that; I can still make fire.

Julie looks like she's getting mad. "Alex! Snap out of it!"

I blink, and see that Nicolas is also watching us, half-hidden by the doorframe, frowning, obviously frightened.

I give myself a shake. "Sorry. Sorry. I... I'm fine."

"What happened?"

I rub my face, and stand, but she keeps staring at me, and I know she won't drop the issue unless I give her some kind of explanation. I'm also pretty sure she figured out I had one of my crazy moments again, so there's no use hiding it.

"I just... I thought I saw something. I'm just tired. I'm going to bed."

I manage to make it most of the way to my room before I hear her voice behind me. I don't turn to look; I don't need to, I can hear how scornful she is very plainly.

"Yeah. 'Cause obviously not talking about it is working out great for you."

I want to answer, bite her head off, even, but at the same time, I don't have the strength for a fight. I just continue walking, pretending I don't hear her.

MAY 3ᴿᴰ, 8:47 PM

I'm sitting on a box in the basement. I came here to escape from the looks of fear and worry Julie and Nicolas have kept sending my way all evening, trying to find a place where I could think and feel a bit better. Except these boxes are full of Mister Lupino's stuff, some of it packed away for longer than the past three decades, and now, I'm thinking of him. I'm gonna have to be the one to go through it. For the first time in a really long while, I'd kill for a cigarette right now.

I hear the door open and shut again, and someone coming down the stairs. Julie walks toward me, wearing a dressing gown over her Pac-Man pajamas, hugging herself. She sits down on a box in front of me, after testing its sturdiness. I say something before she has time to, so that I have some kind of a chance to control where this conversation is headed.

"I talked to Dow about hiring a teacher for Nicolas again. You know, a null."

"What did he say?" She shifts precariously on her box, trying to get comfortable.

"He said that it might not be the right solution. That Nicolas would need to have someone to follow him around forever."

"Hmm."

I look at her. "You don't think he's right, do you?"

"Well, what he can do is pretty... explosive. I don't know."

"What I can do is explosive too. I learned to control it. He can learn too."

"Yeah, but... I mean what if something happens? Something bad? I can't see that we can have someone with him all the time."

I sigh. "Well, what do you suggest?"

She purses her lips, thinking about it. "Well... how about you?"

"Me? What me?"

"Why don't you teach him?"

I shake my head. "I'm not a teacher. I don't know anything about anything."

"That's not true. And even if it were... You know about this. You said it, your power's pretty explosive too, and you learned to control it. I think you're in a better place than anyone else to teach him how to use it. Besides all that, you're his dad."

I run my hand over my ponytail, and think about it for a little while. I guess she's got a point. If there is one thing in the world I know how to teach, it's self-control. I had to learn the hard way. And if the circumstances were different...

"I don't know if it's a good idea, Julie. I'm... things are difficult right now."

She leans her elbows on her knees, frowning up at me. Looks like I'll be having this conversation after all. "How are you feeling?" she says.

I shrug. I know that the real question is whether I'm still seeing stuff, if I'm insane, but I don't know how to answer that. "I dunno. Tired, I guess. Where's Nicolas?"

"In bed."

"Oh. Right. Of course."

She bites her lower lip, and I see the urge to ask on her face. To her credit, she fights it a while before giving in.

"So... these things you see. It hasn't gotten better, has it?"

"No." I shake my head, looking away from her.

"What is it that you see?"

"Things. Most of the time, I hear or see a little girl. Crying. Sometimes there's fire."

She frowns. "That's weird. Does it mean anything to you?"

"Your guess is as good as mine. I mean, it has a familiar feeling. But... nothing I can put my finger on."

"Do you think..." Her expression isn't worried, just wondering. She seems to be getting an idea, and my hopes lift a little bit. "How old is this house? Maybe something happened here, a long time ago, and..."

I let out a long breath, feeling what was left of my hopes and strength go with it, leaving me to feel heavy, and empty at the same time. "No. It's not a ghost."

133

"Are you sure? I mean..."

"I had an expert look at the house. Someone who does this for a living."

She frowns. "Are you sure they were legit? I mean, there's a lot of phonies out there."

I keep avoiding her eyes, rubbing my hands together. "She was recommended by Erik."

"Oh." She looks down, wrapping her arms around herself again. "Well... do you think that... maybe..."

I roll my eyes. If I let her, she's likely to beat around the bush all night, so I just say it for her. I've spent days getting used to the idea, but it isn't any easier. "That maybe I'm crazy?"

"Well, I wouldn't have put it like that..."

"Doesn't change what it is. I'm nuts."

"It could be something else, I guess." She has a smile. I look up at her face, and wish I hadn't; it's full of pity, and I know she's just saying that to make me feel better, like she's given up.

"Yeah, right. Like what?"

"I dunno. Maybe some kind of mind control? Like what Tom can do?" Her eyes widen with delight. "Hey! There's an idea! Why don't you talk to Tom? Maybe he can tell what's happening, and if it's really you or something else!"

"I hadn't really thought of that." I smile, despite the knowledge that I shouldn't get my hopes up. "I guess I can go in the office tomorrow and ask him."

She grins, taking my hand. "Good. I'm sure he can sort this out. Maybe he can make you better... you know, no matter what the cause is."

Even if I'm crazy, she means. I keep my smile, to make her believe that I really think it could work. But the way she said it, it makes me wonder... what if I am crazy, and Tom can't fix it? What'll she do then?

MAY 4TH, 9:34 AM

Tom's office is on the seventh floor. The top three floors haven't been renovated yet, but that's how he prefers it: as far away from other people as is physically possible. As I understand it, his ability's developed quite a bit over the past few years, and hearing other people's thoughts has started to take its toll on him.

I make my way through the hallway. There are no doors, and most of the windows are covered in plastic. There is a bit of scaffolding in a corner, and the floors feel raw, because the carpeting's been torn out. All in all, even though the sun shines through the plastic and it's brightly lit, it still feels eerie and still, like I'm somehow trespassing in a place where humans shouldn't be.

His office is at the end of the hall. It doesn't have a door either, because nobody else ever comes to this floor. I stop in the middle of the hall, trying to brace myself to enter, to clear my mind so he doesn't read it so easily. After three seconds, though, he calls out from his office.

"Just come in and sit down. Ten feet don't really make a difference."

I sigh, and walk in. The chair in front of his desk is pulled up, turned halfway toward the door, as if he was expecting me, which of course he was. It doesn't matter how much I try to hide my thoughts; he always knows what I'm thinking, and if he looks like he doesn't, he's just being polite.

He leans forward on his desk, his lips drawn in a tight smile. "So. You've got a lot on your mind."

"Sort of."

"I'm really sorry about your father." I look away. Of all the things that are going to be nearly impossible for me to talk about, this should be the easiest, because at least it's done, but just thinking about Mister Lupino unravels me all over again. He sighs, running a hand through his hair. "Sorry. I didn't mean to make things more difficult for you."

I glare at nothing in particular, but he doesn't say anything more. I take a deep breath, working up the courage to say it. I know I don't have to, I know he probably knows what I'm here about already, but it feels important for me to say it, like if I need to say it out loud, then maybe I can convince myself that he can't also read how worried I am that I'm losing my mind.

He has the restraint to not answer my thoughts this time, and he just smiles awkwardly.

"So, uh, I guess I've been... seeing things. And hearing things. Things that aren't there. And Julie thought... that you might be able to help me." He doesn't answer, and maybe he doesn't know if he's expected to answer yet; sometimes he has a hard time with verbal conversation. I look at him sideways. "So... can you?"

He shrugs, and tries to smile again, though it's really not convincing; expressions aren't something he's good at, either. "I honestly have no idea. But if there's something wrong with your head, I might be able to find out."

He's probably doing it right now, checking my head, but it makes me feel like I still have some kind of control to give him permission, so I nod. He looks at me, squinting a bit, for a really long time before sighing and shaking his head. He doesn't say anything, though, so I ask him, my tone probably a bit more abrupt than I really want.

"What? What is it?"

"It's nothing. Literally. I can't really see anything wrong with your head. Whatever you're seeing... it's real. To you, anyway."

"What the hell does that mean?"

He makes a face like he's about to tell me I sat in dog shit. "Well... it's not good news, but it's not bad news. I can't tell if you're losing your mind. And for a lot of mental illness, I can't tell when things are hallucinations or not."

"So?"

"So, are there any factors making you think that you're losing it? Like, is there any history in your family?"

"How the fuck should I know?" I grab my head with both hands. I always thought the man my mother made me with was an unusually cruel asshole; what if he was just insane? Does that mean I'm going insane too? Is that what's happening to me?

"Relax, Alex. I was just asking. It doesn't necessarily mean that at all."

"What else could it be?" I'm yelling at him, but I don't mean to. I just want him to tell me it's some super messing with my brain, that it's clear, like a fingerprint or something.

"I guess it could be a lot of things. What I'm seeing is that the things you're seeing, they're real to your mind. That doesn't mean your eyes are necessarily seeing them, but it doesn't mean they're not seeing them, either. The only thing I can tell for sure is that no one is directly messing with your mind. I could feel if it were another psychic messing around in there, unless they were stronger than me, and I haven't met anyone stronger than me yet."

I try to stay calm, no matter how totally unhelpful he's being. "OK, so that's what it's not. It's not someone's superpower. How about what it could be? You said it could be a bunch of things. Like what?"

"I didn't say it wasn't someone's superpower. I said it wasn't a psychic. There are a number of powers that could do something like that. For starters, it could be someone making illusions."

I frown. "Like, images and stuff?"

"Yeah."

"That only I could see and no one else?"

"A little more difficult, but not impossible. And then, there is the possibility of drugs, of course. Hallucinogens, or something like."

I nod. I don't like the sound of that any better. I hadn't really thought of it when Julie mentioned someone else using their power on me, but it kind of hits me, what it means, what drugs or illusions have in common: someone. Someone making me see those things, or something, at least, on purpose. But why?

Tom shrugs, answering my thoughts before I put them into words. "That's a good question. That, and who. Assuming, of course, that someone *is* doing this."

"Yeah." My mind starts racing, and I notice that Tom is listening, probably keeping up with everything I'm thinking, so I stand. "Uh, I gotta go."

He smiles to himself, but I can see there's no humor in it. "Yeah, I get it. Want me to come Saturday?"

I take a deep breath. "No. It's not personal, it's just..." It's hard to explain out loud, but I know I don't need to do it. I don't want anyone I know at Mister Lupino's funeral; I get the whole wanting to support me thing, but having a lot of people I know around me when I'm in pain stresses me out, it never made me feel any better.

He nods. "I get it. Take care of yourself."

I walk away, completely lost in thought. At least, the stress about Saturday is drowning out the overwhelming thought that my hallucinations are caused either because I'm losing my mind, or because someone is out to harm me.

MAY 4TH, 8:37 PM

The house is dark when I get in, and for a moment, I actually think that I am this lucky, that everyone has gone to bed, and I won't need to deal with anyone. But then Julie appears at the top of the stairs, wearing nothing but a t-shirt and underwear.

"Oh, hey." She smiles at me. "How are you feeling?"

"Fine." I hang my jacket in the hall as she comes down the stairs. I meet her at the bottom, and she wraps her arms around my neck, pulling me closer. As she kisses me, it feels like years of tension melt off my shoulders; I didn't even realize I was wound so tight. The next thing I know, I'm turned on like crazy, and following her up the stairs and into the bedroom. I close the door behind us so that we don't wake Nicolas, and she unbuttons my shirt. I push her down on the bed, gently, pulling up her t-shirt, she wraps her legs around my waist, and...

The sobbing starts again. It's not particularly loud, but just hearing it sends a surge through me that knots my stomach, and the ache of desire in my balls is quickly replaced by nausea and a tightness in my neck. Julie senses me freezing, I guess, because she stops kissing me and frowns at me. I smile, try my best to pretend nothing's wrong, but she knows. She always does. She sighs, and lets her head fall back against the mattress despondently.

"You're hearing things again."

I think about lying for a second, but she always sees right through me. I get off of her and sit on the edge of the bed, leaning my elbows on my knees. She crawls up to sit next to me, putting her hand on my shoulder.

"Did Tom find anything that could help?"

I shrug. "No, not really. Not anything definitive, anyway."

She frowns. "Nothing at all?"

I run my hand over my head, grabbing the elastic and letting my hair loose over my shoulder. "Well... yes and no. He said he couldn't be sure."

She starts playing with my hair, running her fingers through the ends. "But he did find something."

"I guess. He thinks... well there's a possibility someone is doing this." I realize as I say it how little I actually believe that. "Like, someone making illusions, or... drugging me."

"Yeah? Why does he think that?"

"I guess he doesn't really think it. I don't really think it, either. I mean... it seems pretty convoluted. I don't know why anyone would do something like that to me, and if it really was someone making illusions for me to see, why only here? Why only me? And drugs..." I shake my head. "I just don't see who it could be. And I don't feel drugged."

She snorts derisively, letting go of my shoulder. "How would you know?"

144

I glare at her, then take a deep breath, trying to keep my cool. I don't know why she's being confrontational about this, but I'm not going to play into it. "I've been drugged before, you know."

She shrugs, looking away. "Not all drugs have the same effect. But maybe you could get tested."

"I guess. I just don't think it's that."

She has a loud sigh. "Fine. What are you going to do about it then?"

"What do you mean?"

"Well, if you don't think it's someone making illusions or whatever, and you don't think it's drugs... then what could it be?"

Now I know she's trying to pick a fight. She knows I think I'm going crazy, it's not like it's the first time we've ever discussed this. "I'm nuts. Is that what you want me to say?"

She rolls her eyes. "You can be so dramatic. I didn't say you were nuts. I just think... if it's in your head, you should get that looked at. You know, call a doctor or something."

"I don't want to see a fucking doctor! What could they possibly do for me?"

"Make you better?"

I turn to face her so we can fight properly, if that's what she wants, but what I see when I look at her stuns me into silence. I expected the pity; it's not the very first time I've seen it on that very subject. What I didn't expect is the disgust I see there, but I suppose that makes sense. The one never is never really far from the other.

It hurts a hell of a lot more than I care to admit, though: I always thought that pity was the worst thing I could see in someone, directed at me, like it made me less than them somehow. But this... Out of most of the people who have been in my life, she was the one I trusted the most. She never had any disgust for me. Not when she found out about my parents, my past, she's one of the only people alive who have ever seen me cry... but this is the first time I ever really felt shame in front of her.

I stand up. "Fine. I'll call on Monday. OK?"

"OK. Where are you going?"

"I'm gonna get some air."

She doesn't say anything as I walk out of the room.

MAY 5TH, 12:33 AM

It wakes me up. Are hallucinations supposed to do that? This time, it's different. It's not just sobbing. They're unmistakable cries of pain. With it, there's also a weird sort of rasping, heavy breathing. I try to ignore it, but it just grows louder and louder, like it's right next to me, and I can't tune it out after a while. I think about waking up Julie for a minute or two, but I don't want to see the look in her face that tells me I'm crazy, especially since I waited for her to be asleep before I crept back in bed. I just get up and go look for it.

It's coming from Nicolas's room again. Why is it always there? I walk to it cautiously, and push open the door, expecting to see the girl again. When I open the door, it isn't Nicolas's room: it's much smaller. It has a single bed with pink comforters, and peeling pastel wallpaper. I recognize it. This scene, the room, the girl, and the naked man grunting on the bed, are all part of the most vivid memory I have of my childhood.

It makes me feel just as sick now as it did back then. He's on top of her. She's just a tiny girl. He's writhing, and groaning, and... when I look down at the girl, at my sister, something strange happens. Her anguished features seem to shimmer, and melt, and transform ever so slightly. The hair gets shorter, and the eyes get deeper, and the face changes shape, just a bit. Just enough for me

147

to see that it isn't Crystal stuck under the fat, naked, sweaty man my mother made me with. It's Nicolas.

I react instinctively and immediately, with even more rage than I did back then; the fire appears in my hands, and all around me, and there's a low, growl-like shout that I feel rumbling in my throat before it makes it to my ears. As I get ready to throw the fire, just like I did, all those years ago, I hear a high-pitched scream of terror coming from Crystal/Nicolas, and I'm suddenly hit by a wall of pain, like I've fallen into a pit of red-hot needles, making all my muscles tense and clench uncontrollably. It's so intense I'm not even able to scream, and I find myself flopping on the ground with the spasms.

It gets hard to tell what's happening around me, but I am dimly aware of footsteps and shuffling and the muscle spasms stopping. The needles are replaced by a different sort of pain, a sharp ache all over my skin and muscles that I've never felt before. I try to move, but my entire body's turned to jelly. I can hear screaming, and sobbing, and I think it's the ghost of my sister going at it again, but the pitch and the sound are very different, and I realize it's my son's voice. Someone turns me on my back, and I think I recognize Julie.

"Alex? Alex, are you OK?"

I make a weird sound in my throat that's halfway between a moan and a gurgle, but I am slowly regaining the use of my muscles. I can feel my fingers twitching, and my legs starting to move. There's still uncontrollable sobbing, and I want Julie to go take care of Nicolas, not me; I'll be fine. Probably.

She lifts me up in her arms, with some difficulty. She's strong, but I'm heavy. As she carries me back to the bedroom, I regain some motor control, and I can make my mouth work, though I sound like Jimmy when he's so drunk he can't walk.

"Nicolas... is he OK?"

"He's fine! He's not the one who got hurt here!"

I need to make her understand. This was my fault. "He needs you... take care of him..."

"He shocked you! He can wait!"

"...be fine. Immune... to burns."

She looks me over critically, pursing her lips. "Well, that's what you always said, but you still look pretty messed up."

The sobs are driving me insane. Why isn't she taking care of him? "...Nicolas..."

She throws her hands up, rolling her eyes. "Fine, fine, I'll go take care of him."

"...be nice."

She snorts and walks out. I close my eyes to just rest a minute. When I open them again, the room is dark, Julie is snoring next to me, and I can still hear the sobs. My whole body hurts, but it's a lot more pliable than it was before, and I can actually move without too much jerkiness. I reach over and shake her awake. She snorts, and yawns.

"Alex? What is it? You need something?"

"Didn't you go comfort him?"

My voice sounds a lot better, but it's still a little muffled, like I'm talking with something in my mouth. My jaw also feels weird. She rubs her eyes and sits up.

"I did. He's fine. He feels bad, but he's going to be fine."

I shake my head. "But he's still crying."

She frowns, and looks at me sadly, and I know what she's going to say before she actually says it. "I don't hear anything, Alex." I sigh, and she smiles, though it's obviously forced. "Do you want me to go check? I could be wrong."

The sobs are so loud I can barely hear her. If she's not hearing them... I straighten, and get out of bed, reaching for my clothes. "No. There's no need. I'm just being crazy again. It's dangerous. I'm dangerous. I should just go."

She sits up in bed. "What are you talking about? He's the one who shocked you!"

"Because I almost accidentally burned him!"

I didn't mean to shout, and I breathe in deeply to calm down. She's so shocked she's stopped moving, and isn't saying anything. I continue to dress in silence, until she snaps out of it.

"You did... what?"

I sigh, pulling on a t-shirt. I wish the sobs would go away, already. What's happening to me? "I hallucinated again. It wasn't him I was seeing. It was... something else. And I reacted to it. So you see? What he did was just self-defense. I'm the one who's dangerous."

"Alex..."

I don't listen to her. I take the car keys and my wallet, but leave my phone, as I walk out of the room, and then the house. I start the car, and as I'm thinking of where I'm going, I hear a faint pop and see Julie's teleported next to me, still in her undewear.

It's a good thing it's the middle of the night, so the neighbors are all still asleep and can't see her.

"Where are you going?"

I shrug. "I dunno. Somewhere where I can crash and not be a danger to everyone else. Maybe the office."

She shakes her head, but I can tell she sees my point, and doesn't know what to say. I don't either, so it's a little while before either of us says anything. She's the first to speak.

"I could take away your power. Just like Nicolas."

"For how long? I mean, your gift is a little unreliable when it comes to duration. It could be half an hour or an hour, and then where would we be?"

"Well, then, I'll do it again!"

"Every half hour? What about sleep?"

"It's good enough for your son, why can't it be good enough for you?"

"Because he's not insane, I am! What if I wake up and I'm bat shit crazy, just like I did earlier? And I can't even tell you're there? What if it's you I attack this time? What if he hadn't woken up and shocked me?"

We're silent again, and I can tell from her expression that she's surrendering, though it doesn't make her happy, not one bit. After a while, she just sighs. "Fine. Go. But if you don't call a shrink first thing Monday morning, I will kick your ass."

I just nod; I guess she's right. It's getting to the point where I'm starting to think the government has the right idea with that

151

registry thing Dow's been talking about. It's all well and good when you're in control, but what about people like Nicolas and me, who can and will hurt people without meaning to?

She seems satisfied with my nod, and teleports away. I sure hope she's right about that head doctor thing. If that doesn't help me, I don't know that anything can.

MAY 5TH, 1:17 AM

I work very hard not to think about what I saw in Nicolas's room as I drive to the office, completely unsuccessfully. Everything I've been seeing is starting to connect, link up, to make some kind of messed up sense. The little girl I saw... I knew she was familiar. It's Crystal, of course. My baby sister. The way she looked when I last saw her, before I left the house I was raised in for the last time. She was wearing that gown when I walked in on the man hurting her. How could I have forgotten what she was wearing? And the fire I saw in the hall. It's all pulled right out of my memories. There isn't a doubt about it anymore, now. It definitely is in my head.

I can see lights in the office windows when I get there, and I can't help but wonder if Dow is pulling another all-nighter. It doesn't seem likely with what's going to happen tomorrow morning, but then again, he's been wound pretty tight with the whole registry business. I feel a bit guilty that I haven't asked about it lately.

When walk in the hallway, I can see the light is coming from his office. I see him hunched over his desk, his glasses down to the tip of his nose, eyes mostly closed, swaying, and I knock on his door gently to wake him. He starts and blinks at me, before looking around himself, confused.

"Alex? What time is it?"

"It's really late. What are you still doing here?"

"Oh. Just... working on some stuff. I think I started to fall asleep. I should go home." He stands up and gets his coat, and his suitcase. As he's walking out, he stops and frowns at me, looking me up and down. I shift self-consciously. I'm wearing my pajama bottoms, and my hair is probably a mess. "Are you OK?" he finally asks. "What are you doing here?"

I shrug. "It's complicated. I just... didn't want to be home."

He makes a face, and for a moment, I think he knows about the things I'm seeing. "I'm sorry I haven't been working on your teacher problem. I hope the fight wasn't too bad. Is she really mad?"

I don't know what he's talking about for a second, and then it hits me. "Oh. Don't worry about it. Julie and I are fine." I see him frown, and realize I really don't want to be explaining anything else, so I shrug and say something that can be interpreted loosely. "I just needed some space."

He nods, looking relieved. "Good to hear. I guess I'll see you tomorrow." He looks at his watch and grimaces. "Or later today, I guess."

I watch him go, feeling like my legs are made of lead. I drag my feet to my own office and collapse on the couch. I stay there, not moving, replaying my hallucinations in my mind, for I don't know how long. At some point I hear noise in the hall, and it pulls me out of my reverie because there isn't supposed to be anyone left here. It's probably just Dow, still hanging around, so I get up to tell him to go home already.

I follow the noise to the kitchen, and I talk without looking as I walk in. "Dow, didn't you say you... oh."

I stop, blinking, because it isn't Dow that's still here in the middle of the night, but Karen, with her hair undone, wearing pink polka-dot pajamas and worn fluffy slippers. I guess it must be because the pink clothes and the long blond hair, but for a moment she looks strikingly like that little girl, my little sister, that I've been hallucinating. I shake my head. I gotta focus; if I get lost in the past, I won't be able to function.

"What are you doing here?" I say.

She chews on her lower lip, looking at me. Clearly, she didn't expect me here either, except I run the place, so I'm the one that has a right to demand things.

"I... Mister Dow said it was OK."

"What?"

"I... it's only for a few days. There, uh... Well, you see, my boyfriend... it's a bit complicated. We had a fight, and..."

"Oh." I run my hand through my hair, and realize I forgot to tie it back up. "Sorry. Of course you can stay here. You got a comfortable place to sleep?"

She nods, looking intensely relieved. "Mister Dow gave me an office with a couch in it."

"Good. That's good."

I sit down at the small table, and the microwave beeps. She turns to it, retrieves a mug, and puts it down on the counter before picking up a hot chocolate packet. She looks at me sideways as she shakes it. "What about you? It is a bit late. Are you having... difficulties at home?"

155

I shrug one shoulder. It's not really any of her business, but I don't have the energy to get angry. "It's complicated. I just wanted to be somewhere else."

She rips open the packet and pours the powder in the hot water. "Well... can I get you something? I could make you a hot chocolate, if you wanted. I like to have them sometimes when I can't sleep."

I shake my head. "You're not on the clock just 'cause you're inside the building, Karen. You don't have to cater to me."

"I know. I don't need to be paid to offer you stuff. You just look like you're having a rough night."

"Thanks. But I don't think I could do the hot chocolate. I'm not a fan of sweet. Unless you have something that'd help me sleep."

She thinks about it as she mixes her hot chocolate with a spoon. "Well... Mister Dow has scotch in his office."

I sigh and lean my elbows on my knees. The motion makes me notice a pain in my right shoulder I didn't really know was there, and I suddenly feel old. I've revised my strict stance on alcohol a few years back, but it doesn't mean that I indulge often at all; still, the memory of Jimmy happily drifting off to sleep in any sort of setting, comfortable or not, as long as he'd had whiskey, makes me think that tonight, maybe one drink wouldn't be so bad. I nod before I've even completely made up my mind about it.

"Maybe I'd have that. Where does he keep it?"

She smiles. "You just go on to your office. I'll bring it to you."

"You don't have to."

"It's my pleasure."

I don't have it in me to argue anymore, so I just stand and drift to my office, where I sit on my couch and wait for her. She soon walks in, carrying a tray with her hot chocolate mug, a glass full of ice, and a half full bottle of scotch, which she sets on the small coffee table in front of me. She takes the bottle, pours the amber liquid into the glass, and hands it to me. I pick it up, and take a sip as she comes to sit next to me with her mug. I've never had anything that strong to drink before, and though it only stings my tongue lightly, it feels like fire going down my throat, and for me, that's saying something. I cough, and have to put the glass down. She chuckles, curling her legs under her and taking a sip from her mug. I look at her. "What?"

"Is this the first time you ever have a drink?"

I shake my head and blink tears away from my eyes, and then I feel the warmth in my chest, and I think maybe it's worth it.. "No... I've had beer and wine before, but never that kind of thing."

She has an unconvincing smile, and looks down at the glass. "Do you drink a lot of beer and wine?"

I shake my head probably a lot more vigorously than I want. "No. I have a drink from time to time, but it's pretty rare. I'm only drinking tonight because I really need to sleep."

The next sip goes down easier, and makes my chest feel even warmer, and I'm already relaxing to the feeling I recognize as pre-drunkenness. I glance over at Karen and see she's still watching me, and I suddenly feel like I should say something.

"Uh, so, thanks for cleaning up my office. You're doing a really good job."

"Thank you." She smiles, and she's kind of pretty when she does it. It makes me realize I haven't seen her happy really often. She makes me think of Lori, or what Lori could have looked like, without the drug habit. I guess it's because of how much like Nicolas she looks. My mind wanders to home, and Nicolas, and my hallucinations, and I need something to distract myself.

"So, uh, Karen... tell me about yourself."

She frowns, and I think I see her blushing. He puts a strand of hair behind her ear. "What would you like to know?"

I shrug. "I don't know. Where are you from?"

"Well... I lived in... Hampton Park, for most of my life."

I think I've heard the name before. "That's one of the suburbs, right?"

She nods. "Yes."

"Your mom and dad still there?"

She shakes her head, sadly. "No. My dad died when I was young, and my mom... well she had a hard time after that."

"Oh. Sorry. What happened?"

"An accident. I don't like to talk about it. What about you? Have you always lived here with your family? Lupino... that's Italian, right?"

I nod. "Yeah. It is. I'm not, though. Italian, I mean. He was my adoptive dad. So I guess we have that much in common." She frowns, like I've said something hurtful. "Sorry. Did I say something wrong?"

She shrugs one shoulder. "You seem like you really love your adoptive dad. Did you have an adoptive mom too?"

"No. I mean, he had a girlfriend, but... mostly it was just me and him." She makes a face. I suddenly realize how that could possibly sound, and I clear my throat. "It wasn't weird or anything. Just... well we were in business together and we got close." I groan. "Normal close. I mean he didn't adopt me until after I turned eighteen. Anyway, what about you? Were you close with your adoptive parents?"

She shakes her head, looking away. "There were a few foster families... I didn't really stay in one place long enough to get close. And to be honest, even if I had, I don't think I would have wanted to get close with most of them."

"I'm sorry." I pour myself another glass. The ice is melting, and the water's mixing with the whiskey, making the drink a lot more bearable.

We stay quiet for a while, and she finishes her hot chocolate and puts the mug down on the table. "Do you ever miss your family? Your real one, I mean," she says.

I shake my head. "It's been a really long time. My parents... well, there's a reason I left. As far as I'm concerned, my adoptive dad, Mister Lupino, is my real family. He's the one who was there for me when my life was the hardest."

"What about brothers and sisters? Did you have any of those?"

I think I catch a glimpse of movement in the hall, and I think I see that little girl with the pink nightgown, that little girl who's my sister. I sigh. "I had a sister. I have no idea what happened to her."

"Do you wish you did?"

I shrug without looking at her, then finish the scotch and put the glass down. "It's complicated. It's not really something I want to talk about right now."

She stands up. "Well I'm not gonna bother you anymore. Better get to bed, it's late."

I frown, watching her she walks out. She seems kind of angry, and I'm really not sure what about. "Uh... Sure, good night."

She doesn't look back and disappears into the hall. I try to examine what I said to possibly make her mad, but I can't figure it out. I pour myself another glass of scotch, and after that one I'm finally tipsy enough to sleep.

MAY 5TH, 10: 12 AM

The house is pretty quiet when I get in. I didn't really want to get up; my head hurts and I'm exhausted, but I needed to come home and change before the funeral. I hear soft clink in the kitchen so I head there, because sooner or later I'm gonna have to face them.

As luck would have it, it's Nicolas who's there in the kitchen, eating cereal. He looks up at me and frowns before looking back down at his bowl while simultaneously putting down his spoon. He stops eating and goes kind of stiff, like he's expecting me to give him crap. I refrain from sighing and go sit next to him. I can see he's glancing at me sideways but still not looking at me full on, like he's afraid of what I'm gonna do.

I clear my throat. "Listen, Nicolas... About last night... I'm so sorry I scared you. I think I was having a really bad dream that someone was hurting you, and I..."

I don't know how to finish that sentence, so I kind of let it trail off. He looks up at me, frowning, as if he wants to believe me but he isn't sure. "You wanted to rescue me?"

I blink at him and run a hand through my hair. It's still loose, because I haven't gone upstairs to brush it or anything yet. "Uh... yeah."

He nods, like he's coming to a conclusion. "That's what Mister Lupino said. That you rescued people with your powers."

I make myself nod. I wish it were that simple, but obviously, it isn't. I'm not going to tell him that, though, because more than anything, I want him reassured that I'm not some crazy guy who's going to kill him. "I guess that's true."

"Then... does that make me a villain?"

I blink at him. He looks dejected and hesitant, and I get the feeling that whatever my response is, it's gonna be really important. It's too bad I have no idea what he's talking about. "Uh... What?"

"You know... A bad guy."

"No, of course not! Why would it make you a bad guy?"

He shrugs one shoulder, picks up his spoon, and start swirling it in his cereal. "You know... 'cause villains are the ones who fight heroes. And heroes are the ones who rescue people."

I scratch my head. I know nothing about superheroes. For the first time in my life, I really wish I had been in the comic books when I was a kid. I'm gonna have to go in carefully. "Well... Don't superheroes ever fight each other?"

He seems to think about it. "I guess they do, sometimes. Like that time Iron Man and Captain America fought."

I force a smile. "Yeah, like that, I guess. But, more important-ly... you were scared, and you were just trying to defend yourself. You didn't do anything wrong."

He pokes at his cereal, which is getting puffy and soggy. "Do you think someday I can rescue people too?"

"Well, sure, I don't see why not!"

He smiles. "Are you going to teach me?"

I frown. The circumstances in which I became someone who takes care of other people aren't really something I'd wish on anyone, especially him. "I'll try."

He puts the spoon down again, staring at the counter. He's picking at one of his nails, and something tells me he's still got something on his mind he wants to say, so I wait for him to get it out.

"So… I guess training me will take a really long time, right?"

I scratch my cheek, wondering where he's going with that. "…I guess."

"So… it's OK if I stay with you a really long time then. You can be, like, my mentor."

That makes me smile. "Yeah! I guess so."

I hear someone clear their throat at the entrance of the kitchen, and I look up to see Julie leaning on the doorframe, smiling at me. He jumps off his stool, running out of the kitchen.

Julie runs her fingers through Nicolas's hair as he goes by her, and then she comes over to the counter to wrap her arms around me. It still amazes me how that simple gesture can make me feel so much better, sometimes. I've never really liked people hugging me, mostly because I grew up in a place where the only touch I got gave me bruises and broken bones, but when she does it, it's always good, and always welcome.

"Hey," she says.

"Hey." I lean against her. "How long have you been there?"

"Long enough." She kisses the top of my head.

"How is he doing?"

"He's been all right. I think you just made it a lot better. How about you?"

"I'm fine. I better go get ready."

MAY 5TH, 2:13 PM

The sky is appropriately gray, and there's a slight drizzle in the air. Nicolas isn't with us, but Julie insisted to come, and I didn't fight her too hard on it, because honestly, I'm glad to have her here. Besides, Luke volunteered to take Nicolas. He had wanted to come at first, but he's been through enough, and since Julie can neutralize Nicolas's ability for a couple of hours at a time, it was a pretty good deal. I certainly didn't want Nicolas to come. Funerals suck, and I don't know that I have the strength to give him the support he would have needed.

There's a lot of people here. Lupino was a well-loved man, especially for what he did. All of his former *capos*, and a good number of their gangs, have shown up to show him respect. The church was almost full, and though most of these guys were shady, there was also Rosanna, and Julie, and Dow, and Jeanine. Jimmy was even there, hanging at the back, which is something, because I know he doesn't usually do churches, he didn't really like Lupino, though he respected him, and he's kind of at war with half the other guys who are here. Things didn't stay stable when Lupino retired, and there's been a lot of dispute, but everyone seems to be keeping civil.

I got the same priest who oversaw the ceremony for mister Lupino's son, over six years ago. He does the ceremony in Italian, and everyone listens, even Julie, who doesn't speak a word of it. The guys each say a little word about him, how fierce he was, how intelligent, how he rose from nothing, how he built the organization from scratch, how he almost single-handedly ruled the city. When it's my turn, I give my own speech, in Italian too, and it's comforting to know that he would have been proud of the effort. I tell people how I was nothing, just a street kid with a gang trying to survive, and he gave me meaning, purpose, relevance.

I don't really talk to anyone at the church. I know I don't have business relations with those guys, not anymore, but a lot of them still don't like me, and I know a lot of them resent the fact that I'm standing at the front of the church, wearing Lupino's name and speaking for him, when I'm not even of Italian descent.

But they nod at me when I step down after my eulogy, and I figure showing me respect is the only way they still have of showing him respect, since it was no secret how he felt about me. I wondered for some years how my leaving the business might affect my tolerance-hate relationship with them. I had thought they would try to kill me, when I left, and then I thought they would do it for sure when Lupino retired, but I suppose I overestimated their dislike. With Lupino dead, I thought, surely, all bets are off, but now that we're seeing each other, it's going all right.

I carry his coffin out of the church along with Dow and some of Lupino's friends, and it's completely surreal. Mercifully, I feel almost nothing when I do it, and for the whole ride to the cemetery, because it's just too bizarre, too unreal to hurt.

The cemetery is full: everyone who was at the church is there, even Jimmy. He keeps his distance, out of respect for whatever cease-fire he has with the other guys, and out of respect for me, but I can tell he wants to come and talk.

The priest does a small ceremony here, too. I can't really understand what he's saying; all the listening's gone out of me, like it's too much to bear. I stare at the sleek black box, hanging over the hole on straps, waiting to be lowered, and I try to reconcile my mind with the fact that it's Lupino in there. It seems impossible; it's just a black box, and it's about to be put underground, buried, covered, hidden forever.

I lift my eyes at the crowd, and see a couple of the guys talking in low voices, and wonder if they're plotting something, but they just nod at me, respectful-like, and it starts to dawn on me that maybe it's not even just about paying respect to the old man, maybe they do have some kind of esteem for me because Lupino chose me; maybe they respected him so much that they hold his choices in high regard too.

Something catches my eye, and I frown. There's a man that doesn't belong, standing out like a sore thumb. He's wearing slack sweatpants, a stained wife-beater tank top, a plaid shirt and a baseball cap. He's also holding a beer can. I look up at him, see the unshaven beard, the beer belly, the straw blond hair, and it feels like all the air goes out of my lungs.

I know it has to be a hallucination again, that it can't be him, it just can't, but that doesn't make it any easier. I try to reason with myself. First of all, he's dead. And second... even if he were still alive, he should be covered in ugly scars. How would he even find me?

He grins at me in that evil way he had of doing right before he hurt me, not in the rage-blind beat-the-crap-out-of-me way he had, but in the sadistic, I-want-to-make-you-regret-being-born way he had about him sometimes, and he lifts his beer bottle at me as if greeting me. As I watch, the skin on his face, his arms, his chest, seems to melt, bubbling, blackening, and cracking, shrinking on his skeleton. It should hurt, but he's still grinning, his smile turning sardonic, his lips burning and curling away from his mouth.

My stomach tightens so badly it's going to squeeze the breakfast right out of me, and I look away. I can still see him from the corner of my eye, even though I'm concentrating on the coffin. The numbing, choking grief is replaced by sharp, cold terror. I haven't felt like that since I was half the size I am now, a tiny kid, defenseless, since that time he broke my arm in two for making his bowling ball fall on top of his beer, accidentally smashing the bottles.

Julie looks at me, and frowns, gesturing with her chin to ask what the matter is. I shake my head, swallowing. I've always been pretty good at hiding my fear, and I have to control it now. I can't look weak, not now, not in front of all these guys, not when it might be dangerous for my life and Julie's. But then again, I've never been this scared, not since I left that house, not in the brothel, not living in the streets, and not fighting for my life against adults who kill people for a living and wanted to add me to their list of hits. I press a hand to my chest, and I hope to shit that whatever I look like can pass for grief.

The priest finishes, and the coffin is lowered into the hole. People turn to me. Julie takes my arm, and gently leads me towards the pile of dirt that's next to the grave, and I remember what I'm supposed to do; I take a handful and toss it over the coffin. I know the gesture is supposed to have some kind of meaning, is supposed to bring me closure, or something, but I feel nothing, except the terror. He's still there, on the outskirts, all burnt up like the last time I saw him. The man my mother made me with.

I concentrate as hard as I can. I'm a grown man, now. Not just that: I'm an extrahuman. I have superpowers, for fuck's sake. I have nothing to fear from this man. I repeat to myself mentally that he's not even really there, that it's just my mind, it's just the stress, and that even if it wasn't, I've fought and won against people who are far stronger, and better, than him.

By the time the others come to shake my hand and give me their condolences, all in a row, I feel numb again, which is an almost welcome feeling. They all go afterwards, in their separate cars, because I didn't organize any sort of gathering after that. There are tensions between them, and while they are religious enough that I can be sure nothing would happen in a church or cemetery, I can't guarantee it won't erupt if they find themselves all together in a restaurant. Dow and Jeanine come after the *capos*, Jeanine kissing me on both cheeks and hugging me tightly. I go through the motions of returning their sentiment. Jeanine doesn't know me well enough to tell that I'm not being sincere, but I see Dow's subtle frown when he claps me on the upper arm. At least, he doesn't say anything.

When they're all gone, Jimmy, who was hanging by himself at the back, walks up to me and nudges me with his elbow deliberately. Does he look thinner? Maybe I'm imagining things. Maybe it's because he let his curly brown hair grow longer, and it's making his head look smaller. For a while now, I've only seen him in those poorly lit dives he loves so much, but now that I'm taking a good look at him in broad daylight, I could swear his cheeks are caved in, and his eyes have dark circles under them. He's smoking a cigarette, and I find myself wanting to ask for one.

"Hey, man," he says.

I nod at him. "Hey."

"You look like shit."

"You too," I say.

He grins, and tosses the butt of his cigarette away. "Thanks. And, I wanted to say, I'm sorry about your Lupino guy." I nod. That's about as respectful as condolences go, for Jimmy, especially when it concerns Mister Lupino. He claps me on the shoulder. "Come on, man, we gotta get you drunk."

169

I pinch the bridge of my nose. That's about the last thing I needed to hear, right now. "I don't think so."

"Why not? It's the perfect occasion. And I thought you'd given up that no-drinking bullshit."

I sigh. It is true that I'm not as strict about not drinking as I was before, but that doesn't mean I get drunk, and right now, after having seen... that man, I feel like banishing alcohol from my life all over again. Jimmy watches me for a while, frowning, and then exchanges a look with Julie, which I'm too drained to read properly.

Julie smiles at me. "Here's an idea. We'll pick up some food, and a couple of bottles of wine, and we'll go back home. Then, you can decide what you want to do. How's that?"

Jimmy doesn't give me time to answer. "I have my whiskey in the car, too. I'll meet you at your place. I guess we can make an exception for just today?"

I rub the space on my forehead between my eyebrows. "Fine. Whatever. Let's just go." I take a look at the place where that man stood, but of course, he's gone. Not that that does anything to make me feel better. "I've had enough of this place."

MAY 5TH, 4:35 PM

When we walk inside the house, it seems too big, and empty, like I could get lost in it. All the warmth it had when I knew Mister Lupino was still in here waiting for me seems to be gone, and the place just doesn't have any of its appeal anymore. Luke isn't here, either, but then, he told me he intended to go somewhere with Nicolas.

Julie and Jimmy seem cheerful enough, and I just eat in silence and let them talk. They seem content with the situation, at first at least, talking easily with one another, laughing. Julie has always been one of the rare people that Jimmy doesn't make uncomfortable, and I'm particularly glad of that today. Once I've started drinking, it's easier to remember what's appealing about it, and the pain and anxiety of Lupino's funeral, and seeing the man my mother made me with seems diminished.

Julie keeps the glasses coming, so soon enough, I'm pretty comfortable in my little hole of misery. It's amazing how much conversation they can get out of the movies they've seen. They like the same kind of stuff, and even go to the movies together often enough, because I don't like to go. Whenever they're together, they're always talking about DVDs which they're trying to make each other watch.

171

I don't know if she thinks I can't see, but Julie keeps glancing at me, like I'm gonna snap and kill them both with a butter knife, or worse, like she wants to talk about my feelings. I ignore her, keeping myself good and quiet. I think I can get away with it, too, like a get out of jail free card, since I just buried the only man I could ever call 'father'. I have an excuse to feel crappy. It's not what's getting to me, right now, of course, but she doesn't know that. Eventually, Julie nudges me with her foot, and tries to get me to smile.

"Hey, handsome. You OK?"

I sigh. "Why would you ask me that? You know what the answer's gonna be."

"Well, yeah, OK, fine, you're not OK. But it seems to me like you're, I don't know, especially not OK."

"Fine. Whatever."

She sighs. "Jimmy, help me out here."

Jimmy shakes his head, raising his eyebrows. "Look, you wanna talk about his feelings, whatever, I won't go against you, but I ain't getting involved."

I'm so thankful for Jimmy sometimes. She rolls her eyes, and turns her attention back to me. "What happened, at the funeral?"

"What do you mean, what happened? I buried Mister Lupino. Isn't that enough?"

"You tell me. You looked like you'd seen a ghost, all of a sudden, for a moment." I frown. She has no idea how right she is. Then again, maybe she does have an idea; she goes on, in a tone that's almost hushed, like she's understanding something. "Did you? See a ghost, I mean."

172

"What are you talking about?"

"At the funeral. Did you... you know? See your stuff?"
She glances at Jimmy nervously.

I don't answer right away, giving Jimmy the time to jump
in. "You still seeing weird stuff? Have you called that woman
Erik recommended?"

I sigh and run my hand through my hair. "Yeah. I have."

Jimmy raises an eyebrow. "Sounds like it didn't go like you hoped."

"No. It... it's not a ghost."

"So, you're losing your shit, then?"

I glare at Jimmy. As much as I love that there is never any
bullshit where Jimmy is concerned, at times, his bluntness is unnerving. Right now, I'm not so much unnerved as I want to punch
him, and I swear, if he says anything else, I will. Julie intervenes, a
little bit more diplomatically than I think I could muster.

"It's not necessarily... that. It could be other things.
We're looking into whether someone drugged him."

Jimmy raises his unscarred eyebrow incredulously. "Drugged?
Into seeing ghosts?"

I shift uncomfortably. Now that I know it was never a ghost,
that it couldn't even have been, I feel like I've been lying, even if
I haven't. I don't know how to tell the truth, though, so I don't.

"...something like that."

Julie frowns at me, taking a sip from her wine thoughtfully.
She stays quiet for a long time, staring at me the whole while,

before asking again: "So... you saw something at the funeral?" I shrug one shoulder, and refill my glass. She frowns. "I saw your face. I know you saw something, Alex. I'm not stupid."

"Well, has it occurred to you that maybe I don't want to talk about it?" I stand, and walk toward the kitchen. If she wants to have a fight, then fine, I don't care anymore, but I don't wanna do it in front of Jimmy. She follows me there, leaning against the counter, watching me. I sigh, probably louder than is necessary, and roll my eyes. "Seriously? We've got a guest. Can't you let it go?"

"It's Jimmy. It's not like he doesn't know."

"So what? So what if everyone knows? It doesn't mean I want to parade the fact that I'm... that I'm..."

She raises her eyebrow. "Losing your mind?"

"Fucking bat-shit crazy is what I was going for, actually."

She has a small chuckle, and I can feel some of the tension between us ease up a bit. "Have you given more thought about seeing someone?"

I sigh. "Didn't I say I'd call Monday?"

"Yeah. But I know you. I know you were just saying that because we were fighting about it."

"As opposed to now, when we're having such a nice talk?"

She snorts and shakes her head, walking out of the kitchen. I think about hiding out here to avoid things getting worse, but then I hear her start talking to Jimmy. I can't really make out what they're saying, but it sounds pretty ranty on her part, so I

174

go back to the living room to try and change the subject. I can't believe she's doing this today.

They fall silent when I walk in, so at least there's that. Julie looks slightly uncomfortable, and it's pretty clear that they were talking about me. Jimmy looks from her to me and rolls his eyes, standing. "You guys are fucking annoying. Alex, if you need a shrink to pull that rod out of your ass, you should talk to Luke."

I shake my head. I know Luke only got his degree recently, but I know I told Jimmy what it was he was studying to become. "Luke's a social worker. Not a shrink."

"Don't they both deal with crazies?"

I sigh. "Yeah. I guess."

"There you go. Same fucking difference. Anyway, I'm out of here. Call me when you guys are fun to be around again. I'm not dealing with this bullshit anymore."

MAY 5TH, 5:38 PM

I'm sitting alone in the back yard, at the small wrought-iron table, staring at what remains of the stain of my blood on the concrete tiles. It's almost a decade old, and it's seriously started to fade; I can probably only still see it because I know to look for it. Eventually, it'll be gone, just like Mister Lupino is gone, and I'll be the only person left alive to remember that meeting, with no other proof than my memories.

The patio door opens and closes behind me, and a few moments later Luke sits in the seat opposite me, the one I sat into all those years ago. He puts his elbows on the table, and leans toward me with an odd expression that's halfway between a smile and a frown.

"Hey, Alex."

I nod at him. "Luke. How was your day?"

"Very good. Your... Nicolas is a great kid. He was really easy to manage."

"That's good." I'm surprised at how relieved I feel at hearing this; I guess I was actually worried something bad might happen.

Luke goes on. "He really looks up to you, you know."

I raise an eyebrow. "What are you talking about?"

"Nicolas. He looks up to you. He thinks you're a superhero, and that you're going to make everything better for him."

"Really?"

Luke shrugs. "Yeah. I guess Mister Lupino spoke highly of you, and Nicolas liked him a lot."

"Seriously? He said that to you?"

"Yes. And there are a lot more things he didn't say that were pretty obvious too."

"Like what?"

"Many things. I think he's getting used to the idea that maybe he won't see his parents again."

I sigh heavily, looking down at the stain. "Yeah."

Luke, as insightful as always, touches my hand lightly to get my attention again. "He doesn't blame you. He blames himself. I know he's hard to approach. But I really think if you talk to him, and you're honest, you might be successful."

"I don't know. I'm…" I shake my head. "I can give it a shot. I just don't know how much use I am these days."

I see him take on an air of concern, and I almost groan. Looks like I'm gonna have to talk to him. He never forces me exactly, but it's always impossible to not say anything with him, and I've learned to accept it over the years.

"Julie told me you were feeling under the weather," he says.

I snort. "I'm sure she told you a lot more."

He nods, not missing a beat. "She did. I wanted to hear about it from you."

I notice a tiny spot of rust on the table where the paint is flaking, and I start picking at it with my fingernail. "What, you want me to tell you that I'm nuts?"

He has a small sigh. "I wouldn't say that. Sure, something is happening, but it could be a lot of things. Even if we were at the point where we jump to conclusions, which we are not, I'm not sure that that would be the conclusion to be had, and that would definitely not be the wording I use."

I roll my eyes at this. I don't know why he always has to beat around the bush. "Fine. I'm seeing things that aren't there. That's what she told you, yeah?"

He nods. "She told me you had thought it was a haunting."

A tiny flake of paint gets stuck under my fingernail, jabbing the finger under it, and I try to get it out, avoiding his eyes. "Yeah. Well I know that it isn't."

"Because of the medium you saw."

"...yeah."

"And?"

I frown at him. "And what?"

"And what else? There's something you aren't telling me. I always know when you're not telling me everything."

I push the little spec of paint too far, and when I manage to get it out, my finger is bleeding under my nail. I grunt in annoyance. "For fuck's sake, what more do you want me to say? How many ways could you possibly need for me to describe how crazy I am?"

Luke, as always, doesn't lose his cool, just has a mild, disapproving frown. "It might help if you told me what it is that you're holding back. Maybe it's what you saw?"

I look up at him, probably a little more sharply than I mean to. I don't really think that he can actually hear my thoughts, but he's so astute sometimes it's just like he can. "How do you know that?"

He shrugs. "Julie said you didn't want to talk about it. Usually, you avoid the most sensitive issues, and they're usually the ones that matter the most."

I shake my head and start picking at the paint again. I just can't look at him when I say it. I haven't really discussed this with anyone, not ever; the closest I came was with Julie, that time in Africa when we talked about our families, and I didn't tell her what happened. What I did. "It's... what I've been seeing... it's from my past. From before... before I met you."

"They're memories? From your family?"

I nod, still not looking at him. "Yeah. From my sister and... the man my mother made me with."

"Are they about anything in particular?"

I frown at him. How does he know there's something specific? I think about the fire, and the blackened body of the man. The faded pink nightgown that used to be imprinted in my brain, but that I had somehow forgotten. "...maybe."

"Well?"

"What, so I need to give you the details?"

He shrugs. "Not if you don't want to. But you will need to talk to someone about this if you want to sort this out. If you're having memories from something specific, it's likely you haven't dealt with that yet, and that's what this is about."

"And you think that if I tell you, it'll go away?"

"No. But, I think your best chance at making it go away is for you to somehow get closure for what happened, which means you need to examine it."

I groan, abandoning the flecks of paint and leaning my head in my hands. "What's the point of growing up and putting things behind you if you constantly have to dig them back up again?"

Luke has a small, half-smile, and he shrugs. "Well, that's the whole point, actually. If you're seeing these things, and they're affecting you that bad... doesn't that mean that you haven't really put it behind you?"

I try to glare at him, but he's right, and I know it. Even worse, he knows I know it. So I just look down at my hands. "I never told you why I left home. I know everyone thinks I left because of what... the man my mother made me with did to me. But that wasn't it." He watches me, not saying anything, letting me go on. I shift a bit; I haven't been this uncomfortable for years. "I had a sister. And he... well he did bad things to her. Worse than the things he did to me. And I walked in on it happening and... Well that's the first time that I ever used my power. I burned him. I think I killed him."

There's a long silence, and I focus on my bleeding finger, picking at the fingernail, making myself bleed even more. I just can't look up at him and see disappointment in his eyes. He's been with me since the beginning of all this; he helped me as much as I helped him, and he's one of the few people whose opinion of me actually matters.

The silence stretches forever, and after a while, I have to either say something or look up. I decide looking up is the better option. I'm not sure I can read his expression; it's something like pity, but he's also frowning, like he's angry. He doesn't seem disgusted, though. I guess it's more like shock.

"What?" I say, probably a bit more impatiently than I intended.

"I'm sorry. I never thought..." He shakes his head. "I don't know why it never occurred to me. It should have. When I think back about it... it was always obvious you were carrying some serious guilt." He looks at me, and I guess he sees something in my expression, because he sighs. "Alex, what I mean is, this is a horrible thing to have gone through and I'm really sorry you had to."

"It's not something I went through, it's something I did!" I realize I'm almost shouting, and I take a deep breath. "And it's something that's in the past. It's over now."

He looks down at the table. "Look. First of all, just because you did something doesn't mean it was easy or that you meant to do it. All of that... it's something that happened to you. Including what you did." I snort and shake my head, and he frowns at me. "Will you stop blaming yourself for everything? Why do you apply standards to yourself that you just don't expect others to live up to?"

"What are you talking about?"

"I'm talking about Nicolas. I know why his parents surrendered him. And I know what he did to you."

"It wasn't his fault. It – "

"It was an accident," he finishes for me. "I know it, you know it. He didn't mean to do it, with his sister, it was the first time his powers manifested, and with you, he thought he was defending himself. Right?"

I sigh, looking away. I don't want to answer because I know where he's going with that, and I can't argue with his logic.

He nods, like he knows what I'm thinking before I say it. "Exactly. If you can think that about him, then you should believe it for yourself too. You were a child."

"I was thirteen. I was way older than he is."

He gives me a patient look. "And how long had you been using your power before it happened?" I roll my eyes, which he annoyingly reads as what it is. "It was the first time, wasn't it?" I look away, not answering. He shakes his head. "Besides which... Think about Kim."

I frown, this time genuinely confused. "Kim? Kim who?"

"Kim. From the home. You've known her for a very long time."

"Why would you bring that up? What does she have to do with anything?"

"She's fourteen."

"And?"

"Do think she's an adult?"

"What are you getting at?"

"You were a bit younger than she is. You may not have been as young as Nicolas is, but you were still a child."

"I wasn't. I was different. I was..."

I don't know how to finish my sentence, so Luke picks it up for me. "You weren't that different, Alex. You're seeing it through your perspective. We all think we're much more grown-up than we actually are. But I was already nearly twenty, and I saw you the same way you see her now. You were strong, and mature, but you were a fourteen-year-old who had been handed a lot more than he could deal with."

"What's your point?"

"I have many points, and I've said them before. First, what happened wasn't your fault. Second... you need to come to terms with it." I look up at him, and I don't even have time to open my mouth before he continues. "Don't argue!"

I sigh, and it's like all the fight drains out of me. "I wasn't going to." And I wasn't. I know he's right. The way I'm responding, the hallucinations... I know that I'm not over it. "I just don't know what to do about it. It was ten years ago, and he's dead. What could I possibly do to fix it?"

"It's not about fixing it. It's about dealing with it. I know that for you, it's usually meant fixing things, but sometimes it's also just about fixing yourself."

"Fine, fine. But what do I do?"

He has a sheepish kind of shrug. "I'm afraid that doesn't have a simple answer. But it might start with stopping running."

I raise an eyebrow. "Running? I'm not running."

184

"You're running from your past. You never talk about it, you get angry when people mention it... you even changed your name and made a whole new family around you."

"I'm talking about it now."

He laughs. "Yes, you've been so forthcoming."

"Whatever. So this is my cure? Talking about stuff?"

"Have you ever contacted your family?"

I blink at him. "What? No. Why would I want to do that?"

"Well... if you want to stop running from your past and face it, maybe one of the first things to do would be to at least find out what happened to the people who were involved."

I lean my head in my hand, staring down at the table. I have absolutely no desire to find out what really happened to the man my mother made me with. As for my mom, and my sister... I didn't really think about it that much over the years. Now that I do, it's glaringly obvious why I don't want to go back.

"Do you really think I need to see them?"

He has a sigh, and his eyebrows do that thing where they twitch up ever so slightly, just enough for me to see the concern before it disappears. "I don't know. I suppose not, but... maybe it would help. Why? You don't want to see them?"

"I don't think they'd want to see me."

He touches my forearm with his fingertips, lightly, before pulling back his hand again, careful as usual with potentially unwanted touch. "It's been a really long time, Alex. You can't know how they feel. They won't even be the same people anymore."

185

I pick absently at the flakes of paint again, and I sigh. There's a reason that people often turn to Luke about things like this: he's usually right. No matter how unpleasant the solution is. I consider the possibility, try to picture myself actually looking them up and meeting with them and talking to them after all these years, and there's a part of me that thinks I'd be better off with the ghosts.

"Fine," I say. "I'll at least look into it."

MAY 8TH, 10:09 AM

Karen is in my office, on the phone, looking like she's taking notes. She looks up when I walk in. "Oh, he just got here. I'll let him know, and he'll call you back. Yes. Thank you." She hangs up, tears out the sheet from the message pad she was writing on, and stands.

"Hey, Karen. What's up?"

"A young lady seems to be needing help with powers she is developing. Mister Dow said you would probably be the best person to handle this. I'll go tell him you're in."

She starts walking out. She's not looking at me, and it kind of seems like she's in a bad mood, so I stop her before she's out the door. "Listen, Karen, about the other night... I'm sorry if things got too personal. I don't usually share with others, and I didn't mean to unload on you that way."

She seems to wait for me to say something else, staring into my eyes as if she's searching for something. I find myself thinking of my hallucinations again, and it makes me uncomfortable, so I look away. She just sighs, and shakes her head, apparently disappointed not to have found what she wanted. "It's fine."

She puts the sheet in my hands, and walks out. "I'll be back with your coffee."

She disappears down the hall, and I glance at the paper. It's an address, a name and a phone number. I put it on the desk, then take off my coat. I've only been sitting for a few minutes by the time there's a knock at my door, and I look up to see Dow walk in, holding a cup of coffee. He puts it down on my desk, and sits. "Here. Karen gave me this for you."

"Thanks." I grab the coffee, and take a sip. It's warm and I wonder how she made it so fast. I put it out of my mind pretty quick, because I'm so tired that I can only keep one thought at a time in my head, and Dow is talking to me.

"How are you holding up?"

"Good, actually. The social worker came by yesterday afternoon."

"Oh! How did that go?"

"It went fine. She said that everything seemed to be in order, and that she would approve us." I have a small laugh, and I shake my head. "It's kind of amazing. I never thought that someday I'd be someone that anyone would just approve to take care of a child." It probably helps that I've been hallucination-free since the funeral.

Dow smiles at me. "Why do you think that? You've been taking care of kids since long before I met you."

"To be fair, Luke did most of the care-taking. I just fought people most of the time. Anyway, you know what I mean. I'm a thug. Well, an ex-thug."

"He's your boy."

"I know. I just... well, you know what I mean. Any luck on finding that tutor for him, by the way?"

He shakes his head. "Sorry. I do have the info you asked for, though. About your family."

I frown. "Oh. OK." I had almost forgotten I asked him to look into this after the funeral. I suppose since I haven't had a hallucination since then, it must have slipped my mind. I guess it won't hurt to just know; I don't have to go if I don't want to.

"I'm afraid I didn't find everything you were looking for, but what I did find was pretty easy to get. Your mother lives in Rockhaven Park, in High Plains. Number 12. She seems to have been there several years." He holds up a file and puts it on the desk in front of me. I don't pick it up; it's kind of thick, there might be pictures. "I'm sorry to have to say this, but... your father..."

"He's dead, isn't he?"

He nods, looking uncomfortable. I don't react, because I'm not sure how to. I've suspected for a while that I had killed him, and it makes me feel a little sick to know I was right. At the same time, the world is a much better, less violent place without him in it.

Dow nods. "He died in an... accident, ten years ago." He glances at me, probably to gauge my reaction. I keep my expression neutral, which isn't difficult because I feel nothing. He goes on. "As for your sister, I'm afraid I have bad news."

That gets my attention. I feel my heart squeeze. "What? Did something happen to her?"

"She was taken out of her home not too long after the accident. She's been in four different foster homes, and one juvenile detention center. She ran away three years ago, and hasn't been heard from again."

I pick up the file and look at it, but don't open it. That means she could be anywhere; she could be dead. She could even have been through Luke's refuge, and I wouldn't even have known how close she came.

"All right. Thanks for looking, Dow. I'll... think about it." He just sits there, looking like he wants to keep talking about it, so I shove the file in my drawer and change the subject. "So, uh, how are things here? I haven't been around much."

Dow smiles. "Good. I think I've finally managed to put a lid on that whole registry thing. Most urgent files are taken care of. If you're going to be back a bit more, there are some things that I would appreciate help with. Did Karen give you that message?"

"Yeah. What is it about exactly?"

"There's a girl developing an ability that's pretty similar to yours. She's having problems coping. I told her you'd be in touch. I figured you'd be the best to do this."

"Oh. That's fine. I'll definitely give her a call tomorrow."

"Tomorrow?"

"Yeah, I was hoping to get caught up on stuff and go home. It's Nicolas's birthday today."

"I had no idea. Do you want me and the girls to drop by tonight?"

"I don't know. Maybe not this time. I think it might be a difficult night, first birthday away from his parents, and all that."

"No problem. Let me know if you change your mind. I'll let Mrs. Wilson know you'll call her daughter tomorrow."

MAY 8TH, 7:39 PM

"Do you like it?" I say.

Nicolas nods, turning it over in his hands. It's exactly the toy spaceship he wanted, but it doesn't seem to make him happy. In fact, we bought him pretty much everything he said he wanted or liked since he came home, but none of it is really having any effect on him. He's not sulking; he's actually being a pretty good sport, and he's been trying to look like he's having a good time, but he keeps looking at the door every few minutes, and every time he's disappointed all over again.

"Yeah! It's great!" He forces himself to smile again, and I feel again like I would rather he was crying. No one that young should know how to pretend they're OK when they're not.

"Oh, hey, look!" I point to the kitchen; Julie is walking from it holding a cake with lit candles on it, grinning. Nicolas perks up at that, and when she puts the cake down in front of him after we're done singing him happy birthday, he actually blows out the candles enthusiastically. I congratulate him and turn on the lights, while Julie starts cutting the cake.

"What did you wish for?" I ask, sitting back next to him.

191

He shakes his head. "Not telling. If I tell, it won't come true."

He looks at the front door intently as he says that, and I have a sinking feeling in the pit of my stomach when I realize I know exactly what he wished for.

The rest of the evening goes well. We all have cake, and we watch the Star Wars cartoon Julie got him on DVD on our brand new TV. He watches it for a while, but he just keeps glancing at the door, and even though I'm not that great at reading people, it's perfectly plain to me how his mood keeps deteriorating as the evening advances. Finally, he sighs.

"They're not gonna come, are they?"

Julie gives me a sad look, and I shake my head. "Sorry. I don't think so. I left them a message yesterday, but... they didn't call back."

He has a tiny nod. "They really don't love me anymore."

I push down the anger I have at his adoptive parents again. "No! I'm sure it's not that."

"Then why didn't they come to see me on my birthday?" He looks up at me, his eyes filling with tears.

"I don't know." It takes all my effort not to tell him that they're just assholes, bad people, and that's why they're not calling him. It looks like they're trying to erase him from their lives; but that's the last thing he needs to hear right now. "I have no idea what they are doing. Maybe they can't call, for some reason. Maybe it's not that they don't want to."

He has a small, unconvinced nod. "Maybe."

"But, you know... we're here. We care about you. We're gonna be there for all your birthdays. And..." I glance at Julie, who's smiling at me. "We love you."

He frowns. "You're just saying that to make me feel better."

"Yeah, I'm saying it to make you feel better. But it doesn't mean it's not true."

He snorts. "Why? You're just stuck with me."

"I'm not, though." I take a deep breath. "You remember what Mrs.... I mean... what your mom told you, that day we met at your school?"

He shifts uncomfortably. "Yeah... that you were taking me away to help me."

"Not that part. The part where she said... that I'm also your dad."

He frowns, looking like he's thinking about it. "Yeah. Yeah, she said that. But what does that mean?"

"It means just that. I'm your dad."

He seems to think about it. "My friend Brennan has two dads, and two moms. One week he stays with one of his dads and the other week he stays with the other. Is it like that? Like, you're my second dad, and Julie's my second mom?"

"Kind of. Not exactly." I breathe again. I can't remember being this nervous, not ever, even after all I've been through. "Do you know what adoption is?"

"Suzie adopted a puppy from the pound this one time."

I guess this is something I can work with. I don't have that much experience with talking to kids, but they're people, just younger, and I know they can get stuff if you explain it well. Plus, I've seen Luke do it pretty often. "Yeah! Yeah, it's like that. Now, you know the puppy wasn't really Suzie's family, right?"

I think he looks amused, despite how serious our discussion is. "Well, no. Puppies aren't people."

"Well, sometimes, people adopt people too."

I let that sink in for a moment. He processes it for at least thirty seconds before replying. "So... what you're saying is... I'm like a puppy at a pound, and you're adopting me?"

"Not... exactly, actually." I look up at Julie, and she nods at me encouragingly, so I take another deep breath and go on. "Nicolas... when you were a baby... The Colsons, the people you know as your mom and dad... they adopted you."

He stares at me, his shock apparent. "What?"

"I'm your real dad. You're my son. When you were little... there was an accident. Your mother... I couldn't take good enough care of you back then. So the Colsons adopted you. And now... I can take care of you again. And there's nothing I want more."

I put my hand on his shoulder, awkwardly, and he just stares at it, saying nothing. There is a long, drawn-out silence, and when he finally speaks, his voice is small, and breathless. "I'm sleepy. I want to go to bed."

He stands, and starts walking away. "Hey, Nicolas," I call out. "You, uh, want me to tuck you in?"

"No." He walks up the stairs silently, not looking back. I watch him go, completely helpless, and Julie scooches over closer to me, wrapping her arms around my shoulder.

"You did great," she says. "I'm proud of you. I think that went well."

"I don't know. I think I would feel better if he had thrown a tantrum, screamed, or broken something."

"I know. I think he just needs some time to process it. But you were fantastic. Where did you learn to talk to kids like that?"

I shrug one shoulder. "It's not that hard." I hear sobs coming from upstairs, and I raise my head. "Do you... think I should go see him?"

She shakes her head. "I think he's fine. Give him some space, and some time to think."

I frown at her. Doesn't she think I should comfort him if he's crying? "But..." I stop myself when I see the small figure standing at the bottom of the stairs, shoulders heaving in her pink gown, under her long blond hair, and I realize that it isn't Nicolas I'm hearing.

Julie follows my gaze, but of course she sees nothing. "Oh," she says softly. "Are you hearing things again?"

I nod, looking away, knowing it's useless to lie to her. "Yeah."

She looks down. "Have you called a doctor?"

"Yeah. I've got an appointment next week." I shake my head. "I hadn't seen anything since the funeral. I thought... I thought it was over."

"I'm sorry." She tries to smile. "You never told me what Luke said."

I shrug. "It's... not important. But he did say something that might help me." I think about the file in my desk drawer. It looks like I might have to look into this after all. "I'm going to take care of it tomorrow."

She nods, leaning her head on my shoulder. "You know I'm there for you if you need to talk, don't you?"

"Yeah." I kiss her cheek. "Thank you." I also know that she won't press me to talk if I don't need to, and right now, it's the best thing she could have offered me.

MAY 9TH, 11:12 AM

The trailer park looks even shabbier and smaller than I remember it. All the same trailers are still there, save for one or two that were already falling apart when I was a child. Some have poorly patched holes in their roof, and most have old tires, trash bags, old boxes, discarded toys, and other garbage all around them. My trailer, or, my mom's trailer, still has those same holes at the bottom that used to let in the raccoons and cats who would steal our food.

I take a deep breath as I approach. I put on my best suit, shaved, combed my hair carefully, but the once-familiar sight of the faded, corrugated plastic siding of the trailer brings back memories of pain and helplessness that make it hard to still feel like a grown man. I hesitate, standing two inches away from the front door for at least five minutes before I work up the courage to knock.

I hear shuffling inside, and it takes her a while to open the door; when it does open, I almost hope that I was misinformed, that she's moved, and that it's going to be some stranger here. I have no such luck. I can see through the torn screen door that she's gotten older; her blond hair is now mostly grey and white, and it's gotten slightly curly: it's hanging almost to her shoulders, but messy and tangled. Her eyes are bloodshot, and have bags under them; her cheeks sag, and have hollowed out significantly. She squints at me, and I'm shocked that she doesn't recognize me.

"Yes, what is it?"

"Uh..." I clear my throat, and wipe my palms on my jacket. "I, ah... can I come in?"

She shakes her head. "Not until you tell me what you're selling."

"I'm not... selling anything. It's... it's me. Alex."

She frowns, and her eyes widen. She finally opens the screen door, and looks me up and down, slowly, like she can't believe what she's seeing. "Alex?"

I nod, trying to smile, but failing. "Yeah."

She steps aside, motioning for me to come in. I don't know what I was expecting; not a hug, she was never one to touch affectionately, no matter the circumstances, but I guess I was expecting some kind of warmth. I walk in, and the smell hits me. Cat urine, and rotting food – I can see there's a slashed trash bag in the corner, its contents spilled out on the floor. I don't know if it's because I was used to it as a kid, or if it's because it's gotten so much worse since I left, but I'm having a hard time standing the stench. She sits down at the small table in the corner. Her dressing gown is frayed and stained, and I wonder how long it's been since she washed it. I refrain from examining the bench before sitting down, trying to remain as polite as I know how.

She lights a cigarette, still inspecting me. "You're all grown up."

"It's been a long time."

She blows smoke out of her nostrils. "Yeah. Ten years. To be honest, I figured you were dead."

198

I look down at the table. A lot of the finish is gone, and I have to fight the urge to keep picking at it, just like I did when I was a kid. "Well... I'm still alive."

"Looks like you've been doing pretty good, too."

"Uh, yeah, I'm the co-administrator at the Lupino-Dow foundation. It's... interesting."

"I heard about that. Freaks with superpowers, right?"

"Um... yeah"

"That explains a lot. So, that's what you've been doing all this time."

"More or less. When I was younger... things weren't always so easy."

She puts out her cigarette, blowing out the last of her smoke. "Yeah, right. You seem to have had a pretty good time overall."

"...I guess."

"You wanna know what kind of time I had?"

I sigh and look down. This is turning out to be every worst thing I had imagined. "I guess."

"After you killed my husband, your father, they took your sister away from me. You tore apart this family, Alex. You didn't just murder your father; you destroyed all of our lives, too."

I stare at her. She's saying those things, and they're awful, but she's not emotional. There are no tears in her eyes, no heat in her voice. She's just cold, and bitter, the corners of her mouth pulled down. It suddenly hits me how different she looks from

Mister Lupino. Their faces are both lined, but his were all in his cheeks, and around his eyes, and they deepened when he smiled. Hers trace a sort of downward pattern, and they fold further with her frown. I may have a hard time dealing with emotion, but I can't imagine being so bitter that I can't even feel anything anymore. I decide in that moment that when I do get wrinkles, I want them to be smile lines, like Mister Lupino, not anger lines, like hers.

"I know, mom. I..." I try to say I'm sorry, but I realize that really, I'm not. I'm not sorry that I killed the man that put Crystal and me through hell until he died. "I wish it didn't have to be so hard for you. You didn't deserve that."

She snorts and shakes her head, and my anger finally cracks through the surface. "Look, it's not exactly like he was father of the year."

She lights another cigarette, and I have to clench my fists together to keep from stealing one of them. "So, that's what you came back for? To tell me how we failed as parents?"

I shake my head. "No. That's not what I'm here for." I try to grasp for a reason that doesn't involve me having to explain about hallucinations, and the ease with which I find it surprises me. "It's Crystal. I'm looking for Crystal."

"Well, she's not here. I haven't seen her in two or three years. Last I heard, she'd run off from her foster folks."

I sigh, discouraged. "Yeah. I heard that too." I stand. "I guess I'll leave you alone." I expect her to say something, protest, maybe, or at least tell me good bye, but she just looks away and lights another cigarette. She hasn't looked up by the time I make it to the door, so I just stop in the threshold. "If you, uh, you know, need anything... you know where to find me."

She has one small, curt nod, still not looking at me, so after hesitating a while more, I get out.

As I'm walking back to my car, which looks uncomfortably expensive in the surroundings just because it isn't covered in rust, my phone rings. I see it's Dow calling. I pick up, getting in the car at the same time.

"Yeah?"

"Alex. I need you to head to Jefferson High."

"I don't know, Dow. I just..."

"Seriously, Alex. I need you there right now. There's a situation."

"What is it?"

"Are you on your way?"

I frown. I've very seldom heard him sound so stressed out. "Uh, sure. I guess I'll find out when I get there."

"Good. Hurry."

MAY 9ᵀᴴ, 12:11 PM

There is definitely some sort of commotion going on at the school when I get there. There are two ambulances, a fire truck, and a bunch of cop cars parked there, lights still flashing. The students seem to have gathered outside, presumably evacuated from the school, huddling together. I park crookedly and get out of the car as I pull out the key, practically running toward the school. The cops gather together to stop me, so I flash my ID from the foundation.

"Someone call the extrahuman foundation?"

One of the cops nods, and lets me through. "She's in the gymnasium."

"Can you tell me what's going on?"

He looks around, apparently searching for someone to delegate this to, but everyone seems busy, so he sighs and starts walking with me toward the school.

"It's a young female suspect. Evidently some fighting broke out in her gym class and she started burning classmates."

I frown. I can see why Dow would ask me. "Is everyone OK?"

"There have been a few injuries. They're not serious, but they could have been."

"Good. What's the situation right now?"

"She's hiding out in the gym. Won't let anyone near her. We'd try sending the firemen in, but we don't know what we'd do with her to keep her from being a danger to the public when she's outside."

We reach the door, and I stop before getting in. "Leave that to me. I'll calm her down, and get her to come out with me. Then I can take her to the center, where it'll be safe for everyone. Is there any way you can get those folks to go home, so it's easier for her to keep a hold on her power?"

"We'll do our best. Do you need some protective gear or something?"

"No. You just stay away. I'll be fine."

He nods and steps away. I walk in. It's dark, except for the flickering light of one neon. All the others seem not to be working. Still, I can see some scorch marks on the floor, and a figure huddling in a corner. It's a young girl, with short brown hair, dressed in red gym shorts, a baggy t-shirt, and sneakers. She recoils and screams when she spots me.

"Stay back! I'm dangerous!"

I stop, and raise my hands in a gesture of peace. "It's OK! My name is Alex. I'm here to help. Can I come closer?"

"No! Are you crazy? I'll burn you!"

"You can't burn me. I'm immune to burns." She doesn't respond to that, but I can see her perk up curiously, even though

204

she's still tense. I take a step forward, opening my hand and producing a flame in it. "See? We've got a lot in common."

She wipes at her face, and I take the opportunity to get closer, very slowly. She leans her head against the wall behind her, and sighs, closing her eyes. I make it all the way, and sit down on the scorched floor in front of her.

"So... what's your name?"

"Jane. Watson. Jane Watson."

"Can you tell me what happened?"

She rubs her eyes, then leans her head in her hands, her elbows propped on her knees. "Well... Sarah kept telling everyone I was a slut. So I called her a bitch, and she pushed me. I pushed her back, and she grabbed my hair, and..." She has a vague gesture toward the scorch marks, and stares at them for a few seconds before looking up at me. "Did I hurt someone?"

I shake my head. "Everyone's fine. And what you're experiencing is not your fault. It started happening to me when I got mad, too." I try to take a closer look, guess her age. She seems maybe fifteen or sixteen. "I was your age when mine started, too. Was that the first time this happened?"

She shakes her head. "No. A few nights ago... I had a fight with my mom, and the book I was reading... it caught fire." She stays silent for a few moments, staring at the floor with a thoughtful frown. I let her think, because it looks like she needs to say something else. "Are you sure I can't hurt you?"

"Yeah. Really sure. Nothing can burn me. I'm immune."

She nods, and looks up at the ceiling. "What's gonna happen to me now?"

"Well, right now, I'm going to ask you to come with me to the Lupino-Dow Foundation for Extrahuman Studies. Do you know what that is?"

She nods, but I see her eyes go slightly wide. "Are they going to study me?"

I shake my head. "Not at all. This is a center created for extrahumans by extrahumans. We're only looking to help. It's a safe place for you to be in until we figure this out, that's all."

"Can I see my parents?"

"Of course. I'll have my associate call them so they can meet you there." She nods, but doesn't stand, so I decide to give her a little verbal nudge. "What's on your mind?"

She chews on her lower lip. "Will they be safe? With me, I mean?"

"Yeah. For sure. This thing is triggered by anger, and stress. It was the same for me, too."

"Then what if I get mad? Or stressed out? I gotta tell you, I'm not feeling particularly calm right now."

I consider my options. I could try to convince her that it's OK, but even if I believed it, talk has never been a particularly strong suit of mine. The other choice might take more time, but it'll yield more definitive results, so I go for that.

"OK. Tell you what. If there's one thing I know well, it's how to use my fire, and recognize when I'm using it without meaning to. How about I teach you at least that?"

MAY 9TH, 1:49 PM

By the time we make our way out of the gym, not only is she feeling more confident about holding back her power if necessary, but the crowd has been cleared. There is still a fire truck and a few cops, but almost everyone else is gone.

I expect cops to stop us on the way out, but I guess Dow must have been busy clearing everything with them while I was teaching her, because they just keep back and let us through. I send him a quick text to let him know to make sure her parents meet us there as we walk to the car.

She says nothing, but bites her nails for the whole drive to the office, and when I park, she doesn't get out of the car right away, just staring at the building. I stay in my seat too.

"You OK?"

She shrugs, looking down. "I guess. Will my parents be there?"

"They should be."

She nods, closing her eyes. She stays still for a few seconds, then takes a deep breath. "OK. I'm ready."

We make our way to the office and, when I walk in, Dow is standing there with two strangers, a man and a woman, who are very obviously Jane's parents by the way they rush toward us when we walk in. The woman throws her arms around Jane, hugging her tightly.

"Oh, Janie, we were so worried! Are you all right?"

Jane starts crying too, and her father turns to me. "This is all your fault! We called you about this two days ago! If you had come like we asked, none of this would have happened!"

I just blink at him, taken aback, unsure how to react, but Dow steps in to defend me.

"I do apologize for the delay, but we are extremely busy, and we do try to get to every request in a timely fashion. It just isn't possible to get to everything right away. I realize that this created trouble for you and your family, but everything is under control now."

The man glances at his wife and daughter, and seems mollified. When he turns to me, there is still a ghost of his former anger in his eyes, but mostly, he seems lost. "What does that mean, that everything is under control? The incident at school... how can that be under control?"

"We have a legal defense unit. Whatever happens as a result of what went on today, we will be able to offer you legal counsel. And we will give Jane the help she needs to gain control of her power and have a normal life."

I stop listening to Dow, watching Jane and her mother talk in low tones. I can't really understand what they're saying, but it doesn't really matter. It's all in the body language. This is what it's like when you have parents who love you. Parents you trust. I feel a sharp pang of envy, and I realize then that even though I expected the result, I really did need to see my mother again, just

208

to realize I really didn't need to think about her anymore, and that that part of my life was really in the past. I am the parent, now, and I know I can give this to my son, because Mister Lupino gave it to me.

I suddenly have the deepest urge to go home, to hug Nicolas like Jane's mother is hugging her, and to tell him that it'll be all right, and that even if I suck at it at first, I'll keep doing my best at this parent thing until I get it right. I turn to Dow; he's done talking to the father, and is looking at his phone. He notices me watching him, and frowns quizzically at me.

"Dow... I think I taught her how to manage for now. Do you think you got this? I have things I need to take care of at home. I'd be back tomorrow."

He nods with an understanding smile. "Yeah. I think we're good. You just call me if you need anything. All right?"

MAY 9TH, 2:37 PM

I'm in a better mood than I can remember being in ever since Mister Lupino got sick as I head to the front door. I feel sort of light when I walk in, and find myself grinning.

"Julie? I'm home!" I take off my shoes, getting farther in. "Julie? Nicolas?"

I listen for their answer, but hear nothing for a few moments, until a sound finally makes it to my ears, and it takes the wind right out of my sail: it's the sound of someone crying uncontrollably. My mind goes right away to my hallucinations of the crying child, but when I listen closer, I can hear that it's Julie's voice. I run to the sound, as fast as I can, and find her in the backyard, cowering in a corner of the patio, covering her head with her hands, eyes closed tight. I throw myself to my knees in front of her, and touch her arms. She cries out, opening her eyes, but seems to settle down, if only marginally, when she recognizes me.

"Julie? What's going on?"

She looks at something over my shoulder and screams, closing her eyes again. I jerk my head around to see what it is that scared her, but there's nothing there, so I turn my attention back to her.

"Julie! What is it? What's happening? Talk to me!"

She opens her eyes, glancing around before focusing on me, and whispers. "Don't you see them?"

I open my mouth to say that I don't see anything, but then she pushes herself back farther away from me, raising her arms protectively, and screaming. "No! Stay away! Get away from me!"

"Julie? Julie! It's OK! There's nothing there! Calm down!"

She doesn't listen; only screams more and more. I sit there, panicking, for a good thirty seconds. Is she hallucinating, like me? If so, why isn't she snapping out of it? What do I do to help her? And where is Nicolas?

I've been in extreme life or death situations many times in my life, but I've never had to deal with something like this, a danger that wasn't something I could physically tackle and disable, and I don't know what to do. I pick up my phone, and decide to call one of the most recent numbers on it, one of the only living people I know that might have the real-life, dealing-with-people experience that I lack. He picks up right away.

"Dow here."

"Dow! I need help!"

"Alex? What's wrong?"

"I don't know! I don't know what to do! Julie's screaming and I can't get through to her!"

"OK, calm down! Tell me what is happening."

"I don't know what's happening! I think she's seeing stuff that isn't there. She just keeps screaming! And I don't know where

Nicolas is!" There is a pause that must last maybe five seconds, but I can't bear to wait that long, and I find myself shouting at him. "Tell me what to do!"

"I'm going to get Tom to come over and meet you. You're going to take a look around the house and try to find Nicolas. He's probably just hiding somewhere. OK?"

"OK."

I hang up, and get up to run inside the house. It feels a little better, having something to do, but definitely not by much. I run through the entire top floor, checking every closet, every corner, shouting his name. I do the basement next, looking through everywhere, even in boxes large enough to hide a kid, but he's not there. By the time I make it to the main floor, I have this sinking feeling that I'm just not going to find him at all.

I run to the tiny office near the front door, where the security monitoring station is. Even though we haven't used them much since he retired, Mister Lupino always had a network of cameras overlooking his house. It's how he knew I broke in, all these years ago, and it's how I hope to see where my son is going. I had turned them back on after he died, just in case some of his old guys wanted to try something.

I sit at the desk, and hit rewind. It doesn't take too long for images to appear; looks like I just missed it, not too long ago. I hit play so I can watch it unfold, and for a moment, I can't breathe.

It's Karen. Karen, carrying my child, to a car I don't know, looking guilty as sin. My unconscious or dead child, limp in her arms. My head is swimming. Why? Why would she do that?

She turns back toward the house nervously and I catch another glimpse of her face. That's when it hits me. How could I have been so stupid? Her using a fake name shouldn't have mattered at all. I know she was a child when I last saw her, but how could I not have recognized Crystal? That's why she seemed so familiar. That's why she reminded me of my hallucinations. I get up to walk back to the yard in a daze.

As I reach the kitchen on my way out, I notice the spilt grape juice and the fallen plastic glass on the floor, and two half-empty cups on the table, and I stop. Did she have drinks with them? What did they talk about? What did she do to Julie? Could she have been responsible for my hallucinations?

The front door opens, and I hear Dow's voice. "Alex? We're here!"

I shout back before stepping outside to join Julie. "In the back yard!"

She's still huddled in a corner, eyes wide and bloodshot, hands clamped over her ears. I go kneel next to her, but she doesn't seem to see me, locked in her mind, rocking back and forth slightly. Tom and Dow walk in through the patio door, and Tom hurries to sit right next to me. He takes Julie's hands. She tries to fight him, at first, but then she relaxes, closing her eyes. Dow comes to stand next to me, clearing his throat.

"I'm assuming you didn't find Nicolas?"

I give myself a shake. Julie is getting help. Now, Nicolas needs me. I stand, and I feel a strong sense of determination. "Not exactly. But I know what happened to him."

I run back in the house, motioning for him to follow me, and guide him to the surveillance room. I lean over the computer, and start playing the video just as he gets in after me. "Look."

He frowns at the monitor. "Is that Karen?"

"Yeah." I sit down, grabbing my head. "In a way. I don't think her real name is Karen."

"What? What do you mean?"

"It's not important right now. How do we find her?"

Dow takes out his phone. I frown at him. "Who are you calling?"

"The cops!" He motions at the monitor. "This is a kidnapping!"

I grab his phone and yank it away from him. "No! Are you insane?"

He rolls his eyes at me. "Look, Alex, I get it. You don't trust cops. You have a past."

"This isn't even what it's about!" Well, it is a little bit, but I don't tell him that because it's beside the point. "She's dangerous. We don't even know what she can do! She somehow took out Julie, and managed to get Nicolas out of here. You can't send in normals! This is my son! If they fail, it's not just them in danger, it's him!"

For a moment, he seems like he's going to argue, but then he just holds out his hand. "Fine. Give me my phone back. I can call in a few favors and run her plates. Maybe we can find something out from her home."

Until I spot her car, I'm almost convinced I'm at the wrong place, because I'm standing outside what looks like an abandoned warehouse. But this is the address Dow got from the license plates, so I suppose it must be the place.

I find a door on the side which is slightly ajar, and I sneak in. It is an abandoned warehouse: there are a few assembly line machines that I can't identify, covered in junk and dust; there are a few crates and what look like rusted-through car parts strewn all over the floor. A banging sound from above me draws my attention, and when I look up I see light coming through the dirty windows of what must've been some kind of an office a long time ago. The door opens to let out a young man I've never seen before in my life. He turns back towards the small room pointing his finger angrily.

"This is fucked up, Crystal. First, you use your power to steal mine to use it to mess with people's heads, against my will. And you know I only came back because you said you were sorry and you'd never do it again. But now you're kidnapping some kid as part of a mastermind revenge plot?"

I see Karen, or I should say Crystal, come to stand in the doorway, her whole body language tense and pleading.

"Norm, come on, don't be that way. It wasn't like I planned for all this to happen!"

"What the fuck are you even talking about? You drugged that kid. How can that not be planned?"

"I just... I don't know what I'm doing. Please don't go."

"I can't be a part of this, Crystal. I just... I can't. This is really messed up. I hope you get some help. You really need it."

He runs out of the warehouse. She calls after him, but he doesn't turn around. She sits down in the rickety metal stairs that lead up to the small room, her head in her hands. I wait a few moments, to see if there is anyone else up there with her, but there doesn't seem to be. After a while, I step out of my hiding place.

I'm silent, and she's not paying attention, so she doesn't notice me until I'm standing at the bottom of the stairs. She looks up then, obviously expecting to see someone she knows, because when she notices me, she stands, her eyes widening. She looks a lot more like the girl she used to be, like this, wearing sweat pants, and without any makeup, and I can't believe I didn't recognize her sooner.

"Alex...!"

I nod, putting my hands in my pockets, trying to appear calmer than I really am. "Crystal." She takes a step back, her shock deepening at my use of her real name. I don't give her time to react, though: I just go on. "Where is my son?"

Her surprise melts into a hostile frown. I've seen hints of anger in her a few times, especially that night that I ran into her at the office, but I hadn't suspected she was capable of this level of hatred and disgust.

"What do you even care?"

I clench my fists, and take a step forward. "Where is he? Is he safe? And what did you do to Julie?"

She folds her arms, defiantly. "What happened to her is her own fault. I guess she's got a lot of ghosts in her past. I just gave her a little something to jog her memory."

"You poisoned her?" The meaning of what she's saying hits me, through my anger. "So it *was* you. You poisoned me, too!"

"Oh, it's always about you, isn't it! You don't give a crap about other people. It wouldn't have been this hard for you to remember who I was if you had thought about me even once since you left!"

I stare at her. "It's been ten years since I've seen you! How was I supposed to recognize you? And if what you wanted was for me to think about you, why didn't you just use your real name and tell me who you were?"

"Because I wanted you to recognize me! You fucked everything up, and then you just left! How could you just leave me? Not even think about me all that time?"

I shake my head. "How can you even say that? You know nothing about me or what I did for all this time."

"I know you've had it pretty easy, with your rich sugar daddy and you big famous career and all the people who love you!"

"You are fucking delusional! I don't give a shit about all that right now, give me my son!"

"No! You fucked up my life, I'm gonna fuck up yours! You took away everyone that I had, I'm gonna do the same!"

"Like hell!" I raise my fists, and my anger is so strong that the flames form an arc in front of me. I push them toward her in a ball, looking to scare her more than connect with anything. She jumps aside, and I take advantage of her surprise to make my way up the stairs as quickly as I can. I only make it halfway up when she gestures, and my foot slips. Completely unprepared, I lose my balance, and tumble all the way down the stairs. It hurts, but I've had much worse, so I stand up right away. The floor under me is icy and slippery, and so are the stairs all the way up to her. So, that's what she can do.

She's grinning triumphantly at me when I stand. "You didn't think I was still defenseless, did you? I can stand up for myself, now."

"Crystal, all I want is to get my son and go back to make sure Julie is OK. I don't know what your problem is – "

"You!" She's screaming, now. "My problem is you! Haven't I made that abundantly clear yet? I'm not going to let you ignore me and pretend that I don't exist anymore!"

"Fine! Then take it out on me! Leave my family out of it!"

"I am your family, asshole!"

"I'm giving you one last chance. Give me back my son."

She laughs. "Or what? You think you can beat me?"

"You don't want to fight me, Crystal." I make fire in my hands again, trying to be threatening, but she doesn't back down. As angry as I am, I don't really want to hurt her, not permanently, at least.

She glares at me, and it's completely clear that she's not going to back down. It looks like I won't have a choice. I raise my hands to throw the fire, but just then, a movement catches my eye behind her, and I see Nicolas, looking groggy and disoriented, and I hesitate just long enough to give her the edge. Water appears at my feet, freezing as it wraps around me faster than I can move, encasing my body in a solid block of ice all the way to my neck.

This isn't the first time this ever happened to me, so I am somewhat prepared for the shock of the cold, which helps, even if it's just a bit. Still, I've never had it happen to my upper body, and the cold and pressure of the ice make my lungs feel shrunken and stuck. I can barely breathe, and my entire body starts to shiver. I make heat, as much and as fast as I can, to break the ice, but she seems to be somehow compensating, because it's getting colder and colder, no matter what I do. She's coming down the stairs, smiling, holding her hand up.

"Not so powerful now, are we? I've learned a trick or two over the years."

Nicolas is half-hiding behind the doorframe, eyes wide, obviously terrified. I try to keep my attention on her, to prevent her from noticing that he's there. She reaches the bottom of the stairs, and she clenches the hand she is holding up. The ice around me compresses, and I can feel my ribs cracking. I gasp, because I can't breathe enough to scream. As she gets closer to me, I can feel the ice creeping up my neck, squeezing what little air I have left out of my throat.

"See? I can crush you whenever I want. I can cover your head and suffocate you. There's nothing you can do to stop me."

"Leave him alone!"

She starts to turn around to look at Nicolas, but she doesn't have time; as he shouts, a huge arc of lightning discharges from his body and collides with hers. She falls to the floor, twitching and convulsing. My heat finally works, and the ice explodes off of me. I fall to my knees, grabbing my sides, trying to catch my breath slowly and with small intakes of air to keep away the worst of the familiar pain of broken ribs.

Crystal has stopped twitching, going limp on the floor in front of me, and I reach over carefully to check her pulse. Her heart is beating, so I dig my phone out of my pocket to call an ambulance. As I'm done giving the address, I look up and see Nicolas, standing in the middle of the staircase, staring at both of us, and I hang up on the operator.

I stand, carefully, trying to make as little noise as possible, managing to only grunt, so I don't scare him with my pain, then walk over to him. He watches me, and it's obvious from his expression that no matter how hard I try to hide how injured I am, I'm not completely successful.

"Are you OK?" he asks when I reach him, and I think that question hurts me at least as much as the ribs.

"I'm fine. How about you? Did she hurt you?"

He shakes his head. "No. I was at the house, and she came to visit, and we had something to drink... and I fell asleep. I woke up here, and..." He looks at her, over my shoulder, and swallows. "Was she a villain?"

I put my hand on his upper arm, trying to be reassuring while still respecting his personal space. "It's complicated."

He looks at me worriedly when I release him. "But she was hurting you, right?"

"Yeah."

"So... it was OK? What I did? Did I help?"

I give him the most convincing smile I can manage. "Yeah. Absolutely."

"Did she want to hurt me?"

I frown. "What do you mean?"

"I heard you arguing. You came here to save me, didn't you?"

"Oh." I smile. "You don't have to worry about that. I'm here now, and I'm not gonna let anything happen to you. OK?"

He nods, and stares at me for what seems like a long time, before throwing his arms around my neck and hugging me tightly. I bite back a moan of pain, and hug him back. No matter how much this makes my ribs hurt, it still feels like one of the best things that happened to me in a long time.

When he finally lets go, he has a hesitant, but heartfelt smile. "*Nonno* was right. You really are a superhero. I guess you're a really cool dad."

I stare at him, trying to come up with something good to say, but all I can do is grin. For the next few minutes, until the ambulance arrives and I have to take charge of things again, I don't even feel any pain.

MAY 9ᵀᴴ, 6:57 PM

Tom is sitting in the hall in front of Crystal's room, playing on his phone. He doesn't look up when I get there.

"Feeling better?" he asks.

"Yeah. How's Julie?"

"She's fine. Dow gave her something to help her sleep it off, but she was already getting better by the time he did. She hasn't called, so she's probably still sleeping."

I breathe a long sigh of relief. "Good. Thanks. So, you got guard duty?"

He shrugs noncommittally, but I know him well enough to know that this is probably the last thing he wants to be doing right now, sitting here with nothing to do, in a hospital full of people in pain, hearing all of their thoughts.

I look at the door, wondering if I should go in. I haven't been able to see how she was, because Dow insisted I get myself checked to make sure none of my ribs had pierced a lung or something, like I wouldn't know, so I have no idea if she's awake or not. Even if she is, I don't know if there's something to salvage.

"Just go in, already," Tom says. "She's open. She's still your sister, under all that resentment. She's just hurt."

I kick him in the shin, really lightly, mostly because being off-balance hurts my chest. "Jerk."

He still doesn't look up from his phone. "Yeah, right. You know you can't keep anything from me, why are you pretending you don't prefer it when I'm straightforward with you?"

"I'm just yanking your chain."

"And wasting time because you're not sure you wanna go in. You don't have that long, you know. Dow and Nicolas are having dinner two floors down, they're already thinking about coming back up to check up on you."

I nod, and walk in the room.

She's alone there, lying on her back in the bed, eyes closed. She's hooked up to an IV and a monitor, and for a moment, I have an uncomfortable memory of Mister Lupino. But she looks nothing like him, so it passes quickly. I grab one of the chairs at the foot of the bed, and drag it so I can sit by her side. I don't have the strength I need to lift it, so the scraping sound it makes on the floor wakes her up, and she blinks at me, then frowns.

"Come to gloat?" she croaks.

I shake my head, sitting gingerly. I manage not to hurt myself. "No. Nothing about this situation makes me happy, Crystal."

She looks away. "So… am I gonna go to some superpowered prison, or something?"

"Depends. You planning on hurting anyone else?"

"What?"

I sigh. "Why'd you do it, Crystal? Any of it?"

"I told you. I wanted you to feel what I felt. I wanted you to know what it was like to lose your entire world in just one stroke."

"What makes you think I don't know what that's like?"

She turns back toward me, sneering. "How could you possibly know? It looks to me like you've had a pretty charmed life."

"It's been ten years. You can't know everything that's happened to me. Yeah, the past couple of years have been pretty good. But I was only fourteen when mom told me to leave, and never come back. I was homeless. I had to do a lot of hard things just to survive."

She frowns at me, looking like she's processing this. "Mom told you to leave?"

I nod. "Yeah. She was pretty pissed. She still is."

"You talked to her?"

"I went to see her this morning." It feels like it was days ago, with everything that's happened today. "I was hoping she could help me find you."

"You expect me to believe you were looking for me?"

"Yeah. Why wouldn't I be? I'd been hallucinating you."

She sighs. "So, it did work."

"What is it that you did, exactly?"

"Norm... this guy I'd been seeing... he has this power. One drop of saliva, and you start seeing the people that haunt you, the unfinished business that's on your mind. Anyway, like I said, we'd been dating, so exchange of saliva happened a lot, and... well I started seeing things. Mostly, what happened around the time you left. And I started getting pissed off. So... with my power, I stole his spit, little by little. And I put it in your coffee."

"That explains a lot."

"When I saw that still, after all this time, you didn't recognize me... I figured you'd just forgotten, or it wasn't as important to you as it had been to me. But I kept seeing you, and dad, and mom, and the fire. So... I decided to make you really notice."

"Why did you take Nicolas? And hurt Julie?"

"I just wanted her distracted while I made off with the kid. Sure, I gave her a lot of it, but I didn't expect her to have so many ghosts."

"Yeah. She's had kind of a fucked up time when she was younger. What about Nicolas? What were you going to do to him?"

"I don't know. I wasn't really gonna hurt him. I just... I wanted to take him away from you, so that you'd lose your family like I lost mine. I hadn't really thought as far as what to do with him."

I let out a disgusted sigh. "He's going through a lot, Crystal. I can't believe you would be so thoughtless. You could have seriously hurt him today."

"Well he seriously hurt me!"

"He was scared! He thought you were going to kill me. Hell, I thought you were going to kill me."

"I was mad."

I raise an eyebrow at her. "You're not anymore?"

She watches me for a little while before answering with a question. "Why did you kill him?"

"What? Who?"

"Dad. Why did you kill him?"

I stare at her. She can't possibly be serious. "I... Crystal, don't you remember what he was doing to you? What he did to us, all the time?"

There is a flash of anger in her eyes, and her voice. "Do you think you made it any better?"

"I guess not. I didn't really... I didn't mean to kill him. It was kind of an accident. It just... I saw what he was doing, and I... reacted. I didn't really know he was dead until I talked to mom this morning."

She looks away again. We don't talk for a while, and after some time I hear Dow and Nicolas's voices on the other side of the door, though I can't make out the words. She turns back to me.

"So... what happens now?"

I shrug. "I have no idea. We make it up as we go, I guess. It's kind of what I've been doing my whole life. It works."

She sighs. "I guess I can live with that."

MAY 9TH, 8:17 PM

Dow checks the back seat after he's put the car in park, and then turns to me.

"How are you holding up?"

I take a look for myself. Nicolas is fast asleep behind us; it's been a pretty eventful day for him, so it shouldn't be a surprise that he's so tired this early.

"I'm OK."

"Are you sure? I mean..."

"No, I'm really OK," I say. "I know I say that a lot, but I really mean it. Things have been tough, but they're turning out all right."

"Tom tells me it looks like Karen... I mean... your sister, she's not going to be a problem anymore?"

"Seems that way. We had words."

"I bet." He clears his throat. "So, uh, listen... I've been thinking."

I frown. "About what?"

231

"About your kid. And about Jane."

I rub my eyes, which makes me realize how tired I really am. Jane. I feel like I met her a week ago. "What about them?"

"It seems like they have the same problem. About going to public school, and needing to control their abilities."

"Yeah... I guess that's true. That makes it more urgent to find someone that can teach them, both the school part and the control their power part."

"Exactly." He has a smile. "Remember when I mentioned that we should start a school? At the Foundation? Well, I've decided to go forward with that."

I think about it. It makes sense. If these two have powers that make them potentially dangerous to other students, then there must be others. If we had a place to take them, then it would take care of the problem. "I guess it makes sense. Have you found someone to teach?"

"Yeah, I think I have."

"Who?"

"You."

I laugh, which turns into a groan because it makes my ribs hurt like hell. "Me? Are you insane? I'm not a teacher."

"After you left, this afternoon, Jane told me how you helped her get her ability under control, at least for the ride to the office. Alex, I have no idea what these kids are going through, what to do with an ability that can be destructive. A null would be even more lost than me. But you, you know how this feels, you've been through it, and you learned how to control it all by yourself. You can do this. You're the perfect person to be doing this."

I stare at him. "You're serious."

"Yeah, I really am. You've been doing a great job, so far, but administrative work is not your strong suit, and I don't think it's making you happy. You're at your best when you're helping people, directly, and seeing the result of what you're doing. And you know exactly how they feel and what they're going through. There's no better person."

I lean my head back against the headrest, thinking about it. He does have a point. A few points, actually. "All right. I'll think about it."

"Good." He smiles. As I reach to undo my seatbelt, he continues. "There is one other thing that you should be aware of."

"What? I've had kind of a long day."

"I know. I'm just giving you a heads up, because I don't want you to be taken by surprise if you see it on the news. But the registry bill has come back."

"I thought it got thrown out in court."

"More or less. I got an injunction. But now they're bringing another bill. A federal one. At least, that's what they're saying."

"Well... can't you do the same thing that you did for the first one?"

"I'll try. But this is a different playing field. And after what happened with Jane, at the school... I don't know that I can stop this."

I sigh heavily. Of course, something had to go wrong. "What does this mean?"

"It might not be as bad as we think. What I'll try to do is get in to work with them to make sure it doesn't go overboard."

"Ok. Fine. Thanks for letting me know."

He nods. I get out of the car, and open the back door to pick up Nicolas. It hurts like hell to lift him, but thankfully he's not that heavy, so I carry him all the way to his room. He doesn't even wake up, and I'm worried for a moment, but when I put him down on his bed, he stretches and automatically reaches for both his stuffed pig and his stuffed bunny, hugging them to himself before drifting off into a deep sleep again.

As I'm taking off his shoes, I hear a sound in the hallway, and I turn to see Julie standing there, her hair in disarray, her face puffy. She's holding a bathrobe closed around herself, and rubbing her eyes.

"Alex? What time is it?"

I walk to her, and hug her tightly. She returns the hug, burying her face in my neck, and it hits me how worried I was about her, how much I needed to hold her after all this.

"It's not late," I say in a low tone. "How are you? Are you all right?"

"I dunno." She steps away from me, but takes my arm and leads me to our bedroom. She lies down, and pulls me to the bed, but when I lie next to her, she just snuggles up to me, holding me. I hold her too, just running my knuckles against her cheek, until she speaks again. "Is this what it was like for you? Seeing people that were dead?"

"I don't know. Maybe. I don't know what you saw."

"All of them. All the people I killed, when I worked for GenEx... They were all there. I hadn't realized there were that many."

234

I kiss her forehead. "I'm so sorry, Julie. You shouldn't have had to go through this. This was all my fault."

She frowns. "What? How?"

"It's complicated. But the short story is... it was my sister. She wanted... she was angry at me, and she hurt you guys."

"She's the one who made you see stuff that wasn't there?"

"Yeah."

"Oh." She looks up at me. "It was hell, what I saw, this afternoon. I..." She shakes her head. "I'm sorry I wasn't more understanding of what you were going through. More patient. I didn't imagine it would feel like that to think you're losing your mind."

I laugh, softly, so that my ribs don't hurt too much. "You couldn't have known. And it's not like I'm particularly patient with you, either."

"How is Nicolas?"

"He's fine. Everything is fine."

"Really?"

"Really." I run my hand through her messy hair. Julie's not someone I usually feel protective of; she can take care of herself, and that's one of the things I love about her. Today, though... I've never seen her be so openly emotional, so vulnerable, and it makes me want to hold her and defend her against everything in the world. Fortunately, despite my ribs, despite how tired I feel, nothing could bring me down. I feel stronger than I remember ever feeling. "He's had a rough day. We all have. But he's fine. I think he's finally coming to terms with the fact that this is his family now."

She settles her head against my chest again. "Well, you are, anyway," she mumbles.

"What?"

"His family. It's you."

I frown at her. "You and me. Family isn't about blood relations. Family's about who you choose to be with. Mister Lupino was my family. You're my family. And we're Nicolas's family."

"Mmm."

I watch her for a few moments, as she picks dust and lint out of my shirt, looking unconvinced.

"Julie."

She looks up at me. She still seems tired, but her eyes are less puffy, and she's definitely more relaxed. "Mmm?"

"Marry me."

She blinks, then raises an eyebrow. "What?"

"I want to get married. I want to spend the rest of my life with you."

She purses her lips. "Are you just asking me cause you think I have brain damage? 'Cause I don't have brain damage. And I'm not crazy anymore. Plus I was crazy for way less time than you."

I laugh again, and it makes my ribs hurt. I put a hand on them, breathing slowly. "I'm not. I really do want to get married. I guess I hadn't really thought about it much, until now, but... you really are my family. And I want everyone else to know that, too." She chuckles and shakes her head, but doesn't say anything. After a few moments, I start getting worried. "So... do you?"

She mumbles, half asleep. "Do I what?"

"Want to get married."

"Of course I want to get married. Dumbass."

She settles closer to me, and within a few minutes, she's snoring softly. I hold her as she sleeps, and for the first time in my life, I really feel like everything is going to be all right.

ACKNOWLEDGEMENTS

Every book is different, and this one was both easier and more difficult to write than the other ones in the series. But one thing doesn't change: as usual, I have a lot of people to thank for helping me see this one through to the end.

First, I owe a big debt of gratitude to my partner Joelle, who's there to cheer me on the good days, and here to pick up the pieces on the bad days. I don't know what I'd do without you.

To my mom, thank you for always supporting my crazy endeavors, and for telling me that I can achieve anything I set my mind to. So far, so good.

To the people who saw this first, thank you for your feedback and encouragements. Marjolaine, Manue, Amy, you've had a hand in making this what it is!

To Frank, as always. Thank you for continuing to make the amazing cover illustrations you have for this series. You have given these books an identity of their very own, and I owe you so much more than I can give.

To all the people who love this series, have encouraged me along the way, and have kept pushing me to work with your enthusiasm: Mélodie, Phil, Evelyn, Eric, Brit, Abigail, Sylvia, Corinne, Philippe-Antoine, Maika, Matthieu, Lucie, Ariane, Evan, Alejandro, Lee, and Andrea.

Last but not least, to the amazing team at Renaissance, thank you so much for your continued hard work.

ABOUT THE AUTHOR

Caroline Fréchette is a sequential artist and author. She has published several short stories, both sequential and traditional, as well as two graphic novels, all on the French Canadian and European markets. She was the editor and director for the French Canadian literary magazine *Histoires à boire debout,* and works in a library. She has been teaching creative writing since 2005, and manages the writing page *Ice Cream for Zombies. Blood Matters* is the fourth book in the *Family by Choice* series. For more information, you can visit her website at carolinefrechette.com.

PRAISE FOR THE *FAMILY BY CHOICE* SERIES

BLOOD RELATIONS

"[Blood Relations] is an action packed adventure that will appeal to fans of fantasy, vampire stories and science fiction. (...) I suspect there will be many [fans of the series]."

> *– Alejandro Bustos, Apartment 613*

"*Blood Relations* (...) is wonderfully written. Alex is a character who is very real and the reader can understand his background and his motives, whether you agree with them or not. This is a story with more layers than you would expect from yet another "vampire story". If you like a hard, gritty story and/or a supernatural tale with a lot of reality thrown in, you will enjoy *Blood Relations.*"

> *– **Geeky Godmother reviews,***
> *http://geekygodmother.ca*

"The writing was great, and the characterization, especially of Alex, was spot on. It's been a long time since I encountered a character who I liked so much. (...) I loved this."

> *– **Majanka, I heart reading book reviews***

BROTHERS IN ARMS

"If you like dark fiction, supernatural, and a good dose of action, then try out this series. You will not be disappointed."

I Heart Reading book reviews

"Alex is a great character. He's complicated, and has many different layers. The story was good, and the writing was spot on the entire time. I was drawn into this book from the first page, and enjoyed it very much."

Forever Book Lover reviews

"Caroline Fréchette is one of my favourite fantasy writers in the National Capital Region. (...) If you are a fan of fantasy I would definitely encourage you to pick up both of these books. The story has a great pace and the strong writing makes them an easy read. As well, Alex Winters is a very interesting character."

Alejandro Bustos, *Apartment 613*

"While I find this series to be a quick read, it is also an incredibly good read. (...) I highly recommend it."

Geeky Godmother reviews

KINDRED SPIRITS

"Since reading the first two stories in the Family By Choice series by local author Caroline Frechette, I've become a fan of her writing. (...) Trust me, you'll fall in love with Alex and his whole world just like the rest of us."

Geeky Godmother book reviews

"Fans of fantasy and sci-fi have a lot to choose from with this fun series. With well written dialogue, excellent pace and interesting characters, it succeeds in creating an intriguing story filled with gangsters, heroes and villains."

Alejandro Bustos, *Apartment 613*

Make sure to check out the rest of the series!

FAMILY BY CHOICE SERIES BY CAROLINE FRECHETTE

An action-packed, fast-paced series about superpowers, crime, survival, and responsibility towards others.

BOOK 1: BLOOD RELATIONS

BOOK 2: BROTHERS IN ARMS

BOOK 3: KINDRED SPIRITS

http://renaissancebookpress.com/2014/09/03/family-by-choice-series/